CIRCLE OF EARTH

THE WITCH'S PROGRESS
BOOK FOUR

LEAH R CUTTER

KNOTTED ROAD PRESS

Come someplace new…
Are you a traveler? Do you enjoy exploring strange new worlds, new cultures, new people?

Journey into the various lands envisioned by Leah Cutter.

Sign up for my newsletter and I'll start you on your travels with a free copy of my book, *The Island Sampler*.

I will never spam you or use your email for nefarious purposes. You can also unsubscribe at any time.

http://www.LeahCutter.com/newsletter/

ALSO BY LEAH R CUTTER

The Witch's Progress

Circle of Air

Circle of Water

Circle of Fire

Circle of Earth

Seattle Trolls

The Changeling Troll

The Princess Troll

The Fairy-Bridge Troll

The Troll-Demon War

The Troll-Human War

The Troll-Troll War

The Cassie Stories

Poisoned Pearls

Tainted Waters

Spoiled Harvest

Bloodied Ice

Tanish Empire Trilogy

The Glass Magician

The Desert Heart

The Ghost Dog

The Shadow Wars Trilogy

The Raven and the Dancing Tiger

The Guardian Hound

War Among the Crocodiles

The Clockwork Fairy Kingdom

The Clockwork Fairy Kingdom

The Maker, the Teacher, and the Monster

The Dwarven Wars

The Chronicles of Franklin

Franklin Versus The Popcorn Thief

Franklin Versus The Soul Thief

Franklin Versus The Child Thief

Contemporary Fantasy

Siren's Call

The Immortals' War

THE CIRCLES OF WITCHCRAFT

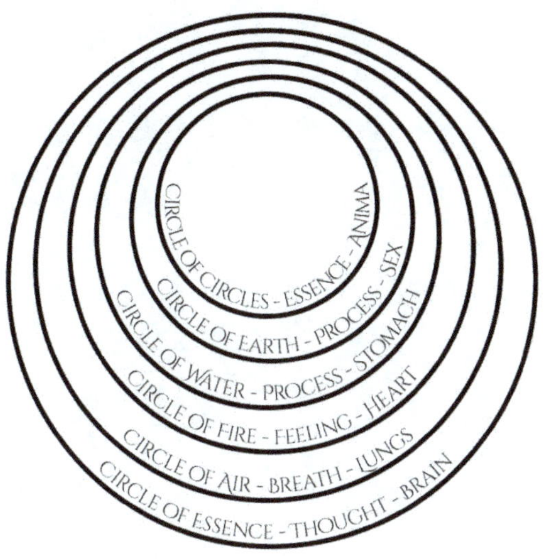

CHAPTER 1

The city of Portland has continued to shine as the only jewel along the western coast that has seen neither fire or earthquake devastate it. Not that there hasn't been threats. The pact with the mighty river god Mulinohana has kept the city mostly safe from flood. I have done my best. But now, we have the threat of all those immigrants, a flood of dirty, unclean scavengers, escaping from the dustbowl and all places east. I would guard the city better if I could. I take their souls, seeking to protect those who were raised here. There is only so much I can do. I know that a small earthquake would terrify them, send them scurrying away like rats off a sinking ship. However, Mulinohana will not allow it. So I bide my time and watch and wait. Sooner or later, my time will come.

Wilson Evermore, Civil Engineer and Protector of Portland, 1932

Tara sat in the backyard of her house, on the porch swing, going over the Portland resiliency report again, the paper commissioned by the local government that studied how well Portland would survive an earthquake. Dew still sparkled on the grass where the sunlight peeked in through the trees. Buds tipped the tops of the roses on the perimeter of the yard, threatening to bloom early this spring. The sole lilac stand in the corner filled the air with their heady scent.

Though it was still early May, the day was already warm. Tara was comfortable in just a peach colored T-shirt and jeans, her brown hair still down around her shoulders. She'd probably pull her hair back and up, as well as change into shorts later..

For now, with her hands wrapped around her hot mug of tea, she was warm enough. That morning, she'd gone for a light Celon black, then flavored it with dried fruit—orange peel and currents—as well as ginger. It felt like the perfect combination of light citrus with spicy heat.

The one good thing Tara had to say about the government was that at least they'd put in effort studying the potential situation. She'd found plenty of papers and websites dedicated to "the next big one"—the earthquake that might end all civilization on the west coast.

Experts agreed that they were long since due for another major quake.

The problem was that while the government had done some things—like moving schools out of old fashioned buildings and into more modern ones—they were merely stopgap measures at best. It appeared to her that less than a quarter of the work had actually been done.

If (when?) a big earthquake hit Portland, the death toll would be astronomical. Plus, only one of the ports had been retrofitted. Neither food nor water would be easily shipped in, as the roads would all be unpassable.

So even after the quake, people would starve to death, or else die of things like dysentery, as there wouldn't be any clean water.

Or, as Tara had read on one of the forums—they were really only a few weeks away from an MCE—a Mass Cannibalism Event.

How was Tara and her coven going to prevent an earthquake from destroying not just Portland but the entire coast? Particularly since the Riprap man appeared set on causing it?

In the six weeks since the Riprap man had sent Tara that map, highlighting the location of a small quake some distance away from the city, more tremors had been reported in those hills. Tara had read at least one official report of increased seismic activity in the area. Were they all caused by the Riprap man? Or had his initial quake created some sort of instability?

Tara had no answers. She'd asked Mulinohana how to contact the Riprap man, or call him forth. As the river spirit was no longer tied to him, the spirit had no idea. However, the spirit did promise to avert what water it could from the city, direct it into smaller channels if the earth suddenly shifted and huge waves threatened to engulf Portland.

However, there was only so much the river spirit could do as well.

A sudden warm spot appeared next to Tara. She put down her tablet and reached down to skritch the ears of Teruko, the fire spirit who took the form of a calico cat. Teruko needed little encouragement, and had already placed his paws up on her thigh, looking for a lap to crawl into.

"Fine," Tara said, pushing herself back on the seat and making more of a lap for the currently tiny kitty. Teruko frequently changed size, going from what Tara considered normal cat size—about ten pounds—down to kitten or up to Maine Coon, depending on the situation.

Right now, there wasn't that much room in Tara's lap, so Teruko had shrunk himself down a little.

"There, is that better?" Tara asked as the cat settled down, purring hard.

Teruko pushed his head up against her arm.

"Fine," Tara said. "Both hands." She gave into the pleasure of petting and skritching a purring kitty in her lap, letting him calm her.

She still didn't know what she was going to do. And it was difficult to imagine that a catastrophe awaited on such a pleasant morning.

But it did. And Tara had to do something about it.

What, though, she had no idea.

As it was Monday, Tara met with her coven that evening, at Hallowed Ground, the homeless shelter that Kaede ran. The evening meal had already been served, and the residents of the building banished to the upstairs rooms.

Tara had no problems entering the building anymore, not since she and the others had helped Kaede rebuild the protection spells that sank deep below the foundation. No one loitered outside the door, as those same spells worked on everyone outside the coven, sending them to other locations for the night.

The tables of the main room had all been pushed to the side and the chairs piled up in the corners, opening the large space up. The building itself had been built back in the 1930s, with the ground floor originally set up as a store, and the upper floors as flats. Shades covered the two bay windows at the front of the room on either side of the door, as well as over the door. The lights came from high overhead, adding a golden touch to the walls and floor. The air still smelled of the spicy spaghetti and garlic bread that had been served for dinner that night, a homey smell that suddenly made Tara hungry despite the dinner she'd eaten earlier.

Kaede was kneeling on the floor when Tara entered, drawing a large chalk six-pointed star on the scarred wooden floor. Ze looked up and smiled at Tara before going back to zir work, still humming and chanting. Ze wore three shirts, all sleeveless, showing off surprisingly large muscles for such a petite, Asian-looking person. Zir skull was still shaved, making zir face seem larger and more fierce.

When Kaede finished zir work, Tara felt the spells take hold, sanctifying the entire building. While she had seen Kaede do this every Sunday, before food service for the homeless, Kaede hadn't necessarily done it every time the coven had met.

However, tonight was a big night. Richard had been keeping track of the tremors as well, and had located one that had occurred late that afternoon.

The coven hoped that by tracking the instability of the earth that they might be able to find the Riprap man.

Tara waited until Kaede stood up and came to join her.

"I wanted to make sure we were safe, here," Kaede explained. "The building will withstand an earthquake, now. I've made sure of it. But there isn't anything we can do about water or food."

Tara nodded. They were going to be seeking the Riprap

man again that night, seeing if the coven could at least find or track him.

The others arrived shortly. Richard, who still had a hangdog appearance, as Jeannie, his girlfriend, had left him shortly after the floods, unable to reconcile her mundane world with the magical one that Richard was pursuing. His heart was healing, but it would take time. Though is large, black, nerdy glasses weren't colored or shaded, they still managed to hide his eyes effectively. More silver threads ran through his black hair than she'd remembered from before, probably from all the energy he'd been expending. He wore one of his many geeky T-shirts, this one saying, *Come to the Math Side. We have Π.*

Lucius and Kyle arrived together. Lucius still looked ridiculously formal even in his tan button down shirt and beige chinos. He'd cut his long silver hair, though, so he looked a little less like his namesake from the movies. Kyle wore one of his dashikis, the green one with white embroidery that looked so good against his dark skin. He kept his head shaved bald and gleaming. He looked more like a hipster and not at all like a high powered law clerk.

Lucius raised one perfectly sculpted eyebrow at the increased protection spells, but didn't say anything. Kyle just nodded and said, "Good. Was expecting trouble tonight."

Ginny arrived last, looking as flustered as always. The new tattoos of dripping water that she'd added to the geometric sequence of triangles down her neck were healing nicely. She'd figured that since she'd survived the floods with the rest of them, that she deserved her own badge of honor. Despite how protected the room and the building were, Ginny still appeared to be surrounded by winds swirling around her, tugging at her torn purple sweatshirt and nipping at the tight black pants with the holes torn out of the knees.

Tara called them all together, placing them each in a point of the star. She started with Richard, putting him with Ginny on one side and Kaede on the other. Richard was the only one without power in the group. She'd found that when she put him beside Lucius, he'd end up falling over tired, as Lucius managed to pull so much more power out of him than anyone else.

She placed Lucius next to Ginny, then Kyle, then herself standing beside Kaede. Kyle had been working hard to overcome his aversion to touch. He'd even talked of someday passing further in, along the circles, and moving from the circle of water to the circle of earth.

However, the circles weren't just about the elements. While the circle of water was associated with process and the stomach, the circle of earth was associated with roots as well as sex. Kyle had trauma from being gangraped when he was in his twenties. Now, twenty years later, he was finally starting to truly leave his experience behind.

Lucius was helping, for which Tara was grateful.

Once everyone was in place, Tara reached out and took Kyle's hand first, just holding on with pinky fingers. Lucius did the same.

Power rocketed around the group when the circle was closed. It always made Tara grin. She'd never felt such a strong circle before, even in Miss Lucy's coven, the first one she'd joined.

Surely they were going to succeed tonight.

"I call upon Areebin, the protector of souls, to set a watch over us tonight," Tara said at the start of their prayers. The names of the gods were many. It had always surprised her that all the covens appeared to call on the same gods, no matter if their focus was on the light and life of others or not. "As well as Samil, the warrior for the people, and his bright shield and spear. Brigid, the protector of the earth, hear our call and help us keep the very firmament stable. I also call on the Hayvu the goddess of the western wind to carry words on her winds, as well as Bonana, goddess of the water, to feed our intent far into the ground. I call on all the protectors, big and small, to help us in our quest. We seek to protect the life of the city and the souls found here. Aid us in our seeking."

Tara took a deep breath, then pulled the focus of the group's magic to her. "We seek the Riprap man. Now."

Richard had sent Tara that map of the area around the latest tremors. It was to the west of the city, in the Tillamook state forest, up in the foothills there. Tara felt herself flying, seeking the trail the sun had blazed across the sky. While her physical body remained behind, sustained in part by the rest of the coven, her mind projected far.

A sharp yip drew her attention. Soot, the first wind spirit she'd called to her, flew beside her. His sleek, black, greyhound body appeared to swim through the air. Soot's eyes had turned golden and he gave her a great doggy grin as they flew.

We seek the Riprap man Tara told the dog, holding her last image of the man in her head for the dog to seek.

She doubted it would do any good. While Soot was great at finding and retrieving things, he seemed to have a blind spot when it came to the Riprap man.

Probably because the Riprap man was able to call the wind spirit to himself, wrestling Tara's control away. Or at least the Riprap man had been able to do that. Tara wasn't certain if he'd still be able to do that or if Tara herself had grown strong enough to be able to hang onto Soot.

Every other time Tara had sent Soot out after the

Riprap man, the wind had returned empty handed. Tara wondered if Soot wasn't able to find the man, or if the Riprap man had just been able to turn the dog away.

However, this time, Soot nodded and nosed to the right a little.

Huh. Where was Soot taking her? She was going to have to drop down soon, find her way through the water and creeks that ran through the area. She hadn't moved within to the circle of Earth—none of them had. So she couldn't necessarily trace trails on the ground.

Dark forest spread out beneath Tara. She heard the hooting of owls. Soot dove down under the dark canopy, leaving behind the open air.

Tara took a deep breath and followed him.

Was this a trap?

Soot swam easily between the trees, skimming over the wide spread of bramble and bushes. Tara had a quick wish that her physical body could do the same. It was a beautiful, wooded area. While it was lovely at night, she wished she could travel through it for real during the daytime, as herself.

The scent of wet pine filled the air. There wasn't enough sunlight due to the canopy of trees for blackberry bramble to take over the area. Tara sensed a river to her right, then had to pull her sensing back, or else she'd be overwhelmed by the number of small creeks and trickles of water running through the ground.

Soot slowed as he left the trees and entered a small, natural meadow.

The Riprap man stood in the center of the open space.

Tara instinctively pulled all the power of the coven to her, floating up in a bubble of power.

The Riprap man looked better than the last time she'd seen him. The rocks that made up his torso were no longer out of alignment. Instead of looking as though he'd been built out of individual stones that had been piled up on top of one another, the rocks had been fused together, giving him a much more cohesive appearance. He still wore pants, perhaps out of a sense of decorum, as he'd been born over a century before. His hat and string tie were nowhere to be seen.

It was his face that amazed her. It, took, had grown much more rocklike. He still had a weak chin and piercing blue eyes, but the ridge of his brow now looked as though it was chiseled out of pale white stone. His cheekbones, also, had grown hard, and the planes of his face had flattened out.

Whatever mischief he'd been up to, it had strengthened him. Not weakened him.

Tara prepared herself for the blast of power sure to rip loosed from him.

She wasn't prepared for his laughter, bitter and mocking.

"I allowed you to find me tonight to thank me again for releasing me from that water spirit," he said. "While Mulinohana gave me great life and a purpose, you have freed me to become who I truly was meant to be."

Tara wondered at the Riprap man's voice. It still held the cultured edges that he'd been born with. However, the hoarseness of it made her wonder. His voice was now rough and gravelly, as though the sound was being made by grinding boulders together.

"And what is that?" Tara asked. "A killer?"

The Riprap man laughed again. "Do you understand the damage that man has done to the wilderness? Can't you see? I remember what this place was once like, before humanity arrived. No, they are the greater plague."

"You protected them for a century or more," Tara pointed out.

"That was my mistake," the Riprap man assured her. "I should have let the first big flood just wipe them out."

"Are you certain?" Tara said. "What about all those beautiful bridges?"

Tara saw a shadow of doubt cross the Riprap man's face. He still had a soft spot in his hardened heart for Portland. "Those people there don't deserve to all die. They need the chance to make the world a better place. They can help. Tearing the coast apart will not solve the problem. It will just make it worse."

"You are wrong," the Riprap man said. "It will take time for the locus to return to strip the corpse of the earth bare. I will be ready for their re-infestation."

"So many innocents will die!" Tara protested.

"None of them are innocent," the Riprap man declared.

"We will stop you," Tara said. She drew more power to herself.

The Riprap man laughed again. He shot down under the earth.

Tara willed herself after him.

Surprisingly, the ground appeared to welcome her. It was as warm as the pool at the Y where she taught classes. The loam flowed around her like thick fog. Boulders appeared like dark clouds, easily passed around. The taste of the rich soil actually delighted her, like fresh morel mushrooms.

Up ahead, tauntingly close, she saw the shape of the Riprap man. He was pale against the dark ground. He looked over his shoulder and appeared surprised at how close she'd gotten.

He dove forward, then shifted to the right, as if that would be an easier route.

Tara followed, though the nature of the soil changed. It grew distinctly colder and she stopped moving as quickly.

She realized that the smooth dirt had turned to clay. Instead of sliding through the soil, she found herself slowing as the clay thickened.

Then slower still.

It dawned on her that this was a trap. The Riprap man planned on holding her here. She didn't understand the magic, as it was merely her projection, not her physical body. Yet she was slowly getting stuck. It was more and more difficult to move herself through the massive pile or clay.

The Riprap man was nowhere to be seen. He'd trapped her, and had taken off.

What was it about the nature of this dirt? Was it the stones mixed in? Tara tried to taste the area, see what it was that was so very different about the clay.

It was wetter, here. Colder. The clay was denser than the rest of the dirt.

The coven far behind her pushed more energy her way. She reached out again, tapping into the water of the clay. Could that aid her?

No, but it was in part why she was entrapped here. Like called to like, and the water called to her.

It was a clever trap, she had to admit. The water calmed her even as the heavy dirt sucked away all her power and magic, keeping her in stasis.

Tara tapped the energy from her friends and violently pushed her way out of the center of the clay pit, heading up, straight toward the surface.

It was only after she'd reached the regular soil again that she realized her mistake.

By destabilizing the ground in this area, she'd just set another tremor into motion.

Tara swam up above the forest and watched in horror as it swayed in a breeze she didn't feel, the ground shifting and waving beneath her. A deep moaning groan washed over her as the very earth undulated. Trees knocked each other over, their root balls suddenly exposed in the air. Birds exploded into the air, screeching their dismay. All the small creatures hidden among the trunks raced out of the area, breaking through the bramble.

The area directly beneath Tara—maybe a twenty-foot radius circle—settled down quickly. She could see the ripples moving out. At least as the area spread the effect grew less. Trees stopped being toppled and merely waved. The stillness of the night returned gradually.

Crap.

She had really been trapped by the Riprap man. He had grown much more dangerous now that he was on his own. Not only could she have died under the earth, she could have done much, much more damage escaping.

Tara tugged on the thread that connected her soul with her body, flying back to Portland and Hallowed Ground. Soot joined her after a short while. He seemed so happy to see her. He didn't understand that she'd just messed up, but good.

The bright lights of Portland just made Tara feel worse. What would happen if there was a huge quake? Would those lights ever come on again in her lifetime? She flew north, over the bridges and up to Hallowed Ground.

The building also appeared to have its own light, safe and warm. She knew that mere tremors wouldn't rock its foundations. Kaede and the others had sent the root too deep.

They couldn't do that for the rest of the city, though. And even if the houses and buildings didn't collapse, that still left the roads disintegrated, as well as the ports.

No, Tara and her friends needed to stop the Riprap man from bringing his tremors into the city itself.

But how?

~

TARA DROPPED HER FRIENDS' HANDS AND TOOK A STEP back, breaking the circle. The air in her lungs still tasted of mushrooms and dirt. Though her skin was dry, she'd swear that the clay still coated her back.

"I don't see how we're agonna stop him," Ginny grumbled. She looked more pale than usual, which worried Tara.

How much of her group's strength had she siphoned off that evening? Richard seemed to be holding up well, but Kaede and Kyle were both listing as well.

"You're not dreaming big enough," Lucius said. He lightly tapped his cane on the floor, drawing all their attention to him.

"What do you mean?" Kaede said. Ze sounded more angry than tired. "We know who it is we're fighting against."

"You're focused on this group, on this coven, being able to contain that madman," Lucius said. He sounded as though he was sneering at him. Then again, he always sounded that way. "Why should it be us?"

"Because we're the ones who broke him from what little was containing him?" Richard asked, sounding just as condescending.

"You misunderstand," Lucius said. "While I might argue responsibility, I would still suggest you're still thinking too small."

Tara made a gesture, urging him to continue.

"While you are all delightfully powerful, I would

suggest that it might be time to call on some other groups as well," Lucius said.

"What do you mean?" Kyle asked, his own expression growing hard.

"You've been associated with at least two other covens," Lucius said with a nod in Tara's direction. "Three, if we might include your former one as well," he added, looking at Kaede.

Ze just crossed zir arms over zir chest and shook zir head.

Lucius shrugged. "So we have connections with two other covens. Why not bring them in? Bind all their power together into one massive, giant spear, and use that to attack? Before the actual earth under the city of Portland shrugs us off?"

Tara swallowed against a suddenly dry throat. She didn't want to have to approach Sheila, who would have gladly thrown her to the wolves, or Miss Lucy as well.

However, Lucius had a point. This threat was bigger than all of them.

In the past, Tara had had to be reminded not to try to fix everything on her own, but to rely on her community.

Maybe it was time for her community to expand to the other two covens as well.

CHAPTER 2

"*I do not care for how the bright lights of Portland have been dimmed by the influx of so many strangers. She is doing her best to feed and clothe all those who are dumped on her shores. There are so many mouths to feed! I relieve her burden, taking souls when I can. However, even the river can absorb only so many. The conservative local government isn't helping, too proud to take the money freely offered by the federal government, content to have the shanty towns sprung up beside the river, Hoovervilles. I have come up with a plan to take care of quite a few of them, all at the same time. To send them into the tunnels and then collapse them all. It would work, if the river god will allow it. He isn't certain, as those souls wouldn't technically belong to him. I am still imploring him, though, to let me do the deed.*"

Wilson Evermore, Defender of the Wealth of the Land, 1933

TARA CONTACTED AALOKA, THE SECOND IN COMMAND OF her former coven. Though it had taken much persuasion on her part, she'd finally gotten Aaloka to agree to talk with the head of the coven, Sheila, and try to get her to meet with them on Wednesday afternoon.

While Aaloka wouldn't make any promises about Sheila actually attending their customary tea and treats, Tara was betting the older woman would show up. She would be too curious not to. Plus, merely sacrificing Tara wouldn't satisfy the Riprap man, not anymore. He was determined to destroy the city he'd spent so long protecting.

They agreed to meet at a coffee shop closer to where Sheila lived, so in northern Portland. It wasn't too far from the beautiful tree-lined neighborhood that Miss Lucy called home.

Like most of the coffee shops in Portland, they had a wide variety of teas as well, though all of them were commercial. Tara settled for a blackberry-hibiscus tea, iced, then made her way outside, claiming one of the tables there. Aaloka approached first, hurrying along the sidewalk. Tara was surprised—Aaloka was actually three minutes early. That never happened.

However, Aaloka didn't seem too distraught. She merely waved at Tara before going inside to get her own beverage, and probably a slice of the olive oil cake, sweetened with honey and lavender. She was wearing a typical suit, this time in a beautiful navy linen, with white piping around the collar and cuffs, with a pretty lime-green shirt.

Before Aaloka could come back out of the shop, Tara saw Sheila coming up the street.

She was glad she had sat outside, even if the day was overly warm, just so she could study the older woman as she walked. Tara hadn't seen her former coven leader in over a year.

Though Sheila wasn't a tall woman, her presence pushed out at least three feet all around her, making on-comers swerve around her without knowing why. Normally, Tara would say that Sheila appeared to be in her thirties, half of her sixty plus years. Today, she appeared much older, perhaps in her late forties. While her gray hair was still completely concealed, the red in her hair had appeared to fade.

It took Tara a while to realize that the difference had nothing to do with how Sheila looked—she wore dark brown contacts to hide the faded color of her own eyes, and her skin still appeared smooth and freckle free. However, her walk was no longer as confident as it once had been. She was almost limping, actually. Had she been in an accident?

There was no question the older witch was still massively powerful. But something had drained her, recently.

Tara stood up as Sheila drew closer. They didn't shake hands, but did stare at each other for a bit. Tara wasn't sure what Sheila saw. Tara had her brown hair worn up in a ponytail, off her neck. Her sleeveless shirt showed off the muscles she'd developed swimming so much recently.

Sheila wore a bright shirt, as always, this one orange with white, red, and pink flowers embroidered around the neckline. The skirt she wore flowed down just past her knees, made out of a bold black and white print.

"You seem well," Sheila said after a few moments.

"You, too," Tara lied.

The old woman cackled at that. "Winter brought a bad fall," she said. She lifted her right leg to the side. Tara couldn't see any bruises or damage to the skin, but she had the impression that the energy that Sheila so effortlessly rode wasn't flowing correctly. "But it will heal soon enough."

"I'm glad," Tara said. And she was. She had never wished Sheila harm, despite how the older woman had kind of hung her out to dry.

Sheila had been working for the good of the coven. If she hadn't, perhaps the entire coven would have been punished with "bad luck" from the Riprap man.

"Are you?" Sheila said, tilting her head to the side to peer at Tara. "Well, you might be," she concluded before Tara could reply. "You were always like that."

Before Tara could ask what the older woman meant, Aaloka came out, carrying two cups, a small pot of tea, and a plate that held two pieces of the olive-oil cake.

"I'm so glad you could make it!" Aaloka gushed. She busied herself setting up the table with all their goodies, handing a fork to Tara, before sitting down.

Sheila sat down slowly, as if merely standing for a while had already led her joints to stiffen up.

Just how much pain was the woman actually in?

They sat in silence for a moment as Aaloka poured the tea for the pair of them and they all tried the cake, which was divine. Tara wondered if it would be possible to redo the recipe using almond or coconut flour instead of wheat.

"So you've survived," Sheila said after a moment.

"I have," Tara said. "And I have my own coven now."

"I heard," Sheila said dryly.

Tara had the impression that the older woman would have liked to roll her eyes at her. It wasn't really a proper coven, not done in the old tradition, where the main practitioner was of the highest circle, anima, essence, and everyone underneath her.

Tara's coven was much more egalitarian. And it had Lucius, who wasn't human as well as Richard, who was all too human.

"I'm not sure what you actually know about the Riprap man," Tara said after a moment. They weren't actually there to be friendly or to chitchat.

Sheila gave her a thin smile. "I know that you've defeated him, at least twice, now. He hasn't taken your soul yet, or been back to bother those of your coven. So I'm assuming he's been contained, at least for a while."

Tara nodded. She quickly explained how she'd stripped him of his connection to Mulinohana, the river spirit, while casually mentioning how she'd bound the river spirit to herself.

That at least got her a look, one that Sheila quickly threw at Aaloka.

"So you've bound a water spirit to you," she eventually replied.

"And a wind spirit. As well as a fire spirit," Tara said proudly.

Aaloka seemed surprised by that. "You're not a hedgewitch," she said. "You've been taught better than that."

"I am both a learned witch, able to pass within, as well as a hedgewitch," Tara explained. She thought that Aaloka had realized that.

"How?" Sheila demanded. "Normally, a witch cannot progress along both paths."

"Why not?" Tara asked.

"The powers aren't complementary," Aaloka said, as if

explaining something to someone much younger than she was.

Tara merely shrugged. "They seem to be working together fine," she said. Though she wasn't about to admit that she occasionally had difficulty now when it came to creating potions and sachets.

"But despite that, despite the power of our group, the Riprap man is still a threat," Tara said.

"You took away his spirit companion," Sheila said.

"No, not exactly," Tara said. "You see, the Riprap man is associated with the earth. With rocks and stones. The riprap at the footing of a pier." She paused, considering her words. "He'd been bound to a river spirit. Something that actually deformed him over all those years."

She made herself say the conclusion she'd come to after a while. "The river spirit actually contained him. Confined him. And now, he has nothing that's holding him back."

"What does that have to do with us?" Sheila said. She had sat back and was starting to look defensive.

Tara wondered if the older witch already had a sachet in her purse for extra protection that she was itching to bring out.

"He protected the city of Portland for over a century," Tara said. "Killing witches to renew his pact with the river spirit. Now, he wants nothing more than to destroy the entire place. Wipe it out of existence."

"How?" Aaloka asked. "He can't flood the city any more, can he?"

"Mulinohana won't allow that," Tara said. "The river spirit. No, he's now calling on his natural abilities, to use rock and stone, the very land against us." She took a deep breath. "Earthquakes." The more she'd studied the potential, the more nervous Tara had grown, and she now started when a truck rumbled by.

Aaloka gasped.

"Brigid protect us," Sheila breathed out.

"Is he behind the increased tremors in the area?" Aaloka asked. "I saw something on the news last night about it, an unexpected fault letting loose in the Tillamook forest."

Tara nodded, aware that it had actually been her that had caused that latest accident. "Yes. He's been experimenting, causing a bunch of little earthquakes all around the city. We can't figure out why—possibly shaking out the cracks so that the big one will hit us all the harder."

Sheila had actually grown pale at the news. At least they were taking her seriously.

"We have to stop him," Tara said. "My group—as strong as it is—isn't strong enough to handle him on his own."

Tara didn't like the sly look that came over Sheila's face. "So you want to work together," she said. She gave Tara a smile that looked like the cat who'd just eaten all the cream.

"Yes," Tara said. "I'd like to bring your coven, and Miss Lucy's coven, and ours together to see if we can destroy the Riprap man once and for all."

Aaloka exchanged another look with Sheila. "So why not bind him instead?" she said. "You've brought over other powerful spirits."

Tara shrugged. "No binding lasts forever." She'd discovered that when the being bound to the sea wall finally escaped. "I don't want to create a problem that must be solved by a future generation."

"That makes sense," Sheila said slowly. "Do you know how to track him?"

"Maybe," Tara said. "We've been tracking the tremors, and following him back to them."

Sheila nodded. "That would make it difficult, then. Having to wait until a tremor was reported before being able to find him."

"Could you lay a trap for him instead?" Aaloka asked.

Tara kept her sigh to herself. She knew that her former mentor didn't understand what she was asking. However, Tara had considered that aspect herself already.

"We might be able to entice him into an area," Tara said slowly. At the nods she received from the other witches. "It's just that he would be coming after me, myself."

"We could work with that," Sheila said.

Tara didn't like how much that made her feel like bait. Dead bait.

"We'll see what we can do," Tara said after a bit. "But you'd be amenable to working together? Bringing the covens together?"

Sheila and Aaloka looked at each other. Tara wasn't certain what their look was saying, what silent words they exchanged. However, eventually Aaloka nodded.

"Yes, I think we could figure something out," Sheila purred.

Tara knew in her heart of hearts that agreeing to this was likely to put her, and possibly all of Portland into more danger, not less.

Still, she didn't see what else she could do.

She agreed, and the two witches shook hands on it.

～

Tara had called Miss Lucy to set up an appointment with her. It surprised her when the older woman suggested that they have lunch together, instead of meeting at her house. Tara had rarely seen Miss Lucy in a social setting, and not at her house instead.

But Tara agreed to meet her at a club that was south of the city. She looked the place up online, whistling softly at how upscale it appeared to be.

Jeans and a T-shirt were not going to do.

Instead, Tara wore one of her nicer dresses made out of a purple cotton with a pattern of large white irises on it. She actually got one of her housemates to braid her hair for her. She didn't bother with makeup—that was one step too far. She did put on a pair of nice black low heels, and carried a soft white knitted shawl.

Normally, Tara took the bus or MAX everywhere. Of course, there were no stops anywhere near the club. Those kinds of people wouldn't be welcome. Though she couldn't really afford it, Tara took a shared-ride taxi up, spending the entire time chatting with the driver about his brother back in Pakistan and how you had to work so hard here in America.

Expensive cars lined the street close to the club. Trees, too. Older houses sat back from the road, the yards covered in immaculate yards. However, Tara could smell the river as soon as she stepped out from the car. She knew she didn't have a lot of time, but she still walked north of the building, trying to catch a glimpse of the water.

Water had always been her element. She found that now that she'd bound a water spirit, she spent even more time near it. It called to her anytime she caught a scent of it and she frequently dreamed of floating on the waves, carried this way and that by the currents.

The sun shone bright down on the gray waters. Green

banks rose up on both sides. Red-winged blackbirds called cheerily to each other, and she heard the industrial buzzing of bees traversing the blackberry bushes. The water itself smelled of the sea today, salty and moist.

After paying her respects, Tara made her way back to the dark club. She had to pause once she stepped inside out of the bright sunlight.

The hostess standing behind the reception area waited patiently for Tara to blink her way to clarity, not bothering to speak until Tara took a few more steps inside the room.

The front hallway was closed in, like a closet made out of fancy wood paneling. The reception desk was also made out of a heavy wood, with a discrete light shining down on the desk. Muted conversations rose up from either side, the restaurant apparently spread out to both sides.

"May I help you?" the hostess said. She wore a beautiful golden-silk blouse that probably would have cost Tara half a month's rent. Her teeth were perfect, as was her hair and makeup. Probably took her three hours every morning just to make herself look presentable.

"I'm here for lunch," Tara said baldly.

"Do you have a reservation?" the hostess asked, already looking down her nose. Well, as much as she could, as Tara stood at least half a head taller than her.

"Yes," Tara said. "Miss Lucy," she added after a moment. "Lucy Talbot."

"Oh!" the hostess said.

Tara grinned at the girl's reaction. Obviously, she hadn't expected someone as down and out as Tara to be meeting with such a high-powered client.

"Right this way," the girl said, hurrying off.

Tara continued to grin as the girl led her to a booth off to the left. Past the small bar, the room opened up. Large windows lined the wall, all overlooking the river. Miss

Lucy sat in a small booth near the middle of the room, backlit by the bright sunlight.

She stood as Tara drew closer, leaning over the table to air-kiss both of Tara's cheeks. "So good of you to come to lunch with me, my dear," Miss Lucy said.

Tara didn't reply despite her confusion. She'd been the one to set up the meeting.

However, based on the gaping expression on the face of the hostess, evidently Miss Lucy had been setting her up.

After Tara was seated, a waiter came up to take their drinks order, with Tara getting plain water with lemon while Miss Lucy got sparkling water with a twist of lime.

"It's so good to see you," Miss Lucy told Tara. "You're looking well. Strong," she added. "You seem to be coming into your own."

"Thank you," Tara said. "You look good too." And Miss Lucy did. Her skin was a light colored brown, and she always wore hats to protect her face from developing freckles across her nose. She wore her black hair straightened, with a slight curl above the shoulders of her exquisite lemon-yellow silk top, with pearl buttons down the front. Her broad lips curved in a generous smile.

Miss Lucy was also in her sixties. However, unlike Sheila, she'd never tried to hide her age. Her brown eyes were faded, and obvious wrinkles crinkled around her mouth and the edges of her eyes. Power still emanated from her.

Tara hadn't seen Miss Lucy in a year, not since her former teacher had helped her reach the room of one of the witches who'd been buried at the foot of the pier of a bridge. They'd talked on the phone a couple of times, though not in depth.

"Tell me everything," Miss Lucy demanded after they'd ordered food.

Tara nodded and began, starting with the first battle she'd had with the Riprap man.

"I have a question for you darling," Miss Lucy said, interrupting Tara a minute or so after she'd started. "Where's that quiet coming from?"

Tara looked around, unsure what Miss Lucy was referring to. "Quiet?" she asked. She peered out, over the rest of the restaurant. "Oh! That's from me," Tara said. "The hedgewitch magic."

Miss Lucy frowned at her. "Hedgewitch?"

Tara shrugged. "I seem to have both," she said. "The ability to do learned magic, as well as natural."

"And the quiet wasn't something you spelled, was it?" Miss Lucy said as the noise in the restaurant started to trickle into the bubble that Tara had originally, accidently formed.

"It isn't," Tara admitted. "It just happens sometimes."

"That's always the problem with that sort of magic," Miss Lucy said, obviously disapproving. "It just happens. No control, whatsoever. I thought you were better trained than that."

Tara grimaced. "I've kept up my training," she said. "I've been passed within, a witch of the circle of water."

Miss Lucy nodded. "Good. Good! I always thought you should be at that level," she said. "You take nicely to water."

"Yes," Tara said. "I've bound a water spirit to me," she added.

Miss Lucy blinked, surprised. "Darling, you really do have to tell me all about it. Now, continue."

Tara smiled and continued talking. The sounds of the rest of the restaurant faded away again as Tara told her old mentor everything, all the battles she'd had with the Riprap man, all the successes she'd had as well.

By the time she'd finished, they were finished with their meal and contemplating dessert. Miss Lucy insisted that they split the flourless chocolate torte with raspberry ice cream.

"I assume that you're here for something other than telling me your tales," Miss Lucy said.

"Yes," Tara said. "We need your help. The help of your coven. We need more power than what we have to defeat the Riprap man. We'd like to have a group of covens, coming together, our power converging."

Miss Lucy nodded. "And you've already asked Sheila, haven't you?"

"I did," Tara said, surprised that Miss Lucy would know that.

"She will try to take over your coven," Miss Lucy warned.

Tara snorted. "She can try."

Miss Lucy tilted her head to the side to peer at Tara. "Interesting," she said. "You've grown into your powers. Much more than I would have expected."

"Did you ever suspect that I had hedgewitch powers?" Tara asked. She'd wondered that for a long while, actually.

Miss Lucy laughed. "All witches have the potential for using hedgewitch powers," she said. "They all have the ability. They just never tap into them."

"Really?" Tara said, surprised. She'd thought that there were actually two different breeds of witches.

"Tell me, which do you find easier?" Miss Lucy said.

Tara thought for a moment before she replied. She never would have admitted this to anyone else. Possibly not even her coven.

"I'm starting to have more difficulty with the schooled

witch parts," Tara finally confessed. It was actually the first time she'd spoken the words out loud.

"I'm not surprised," Miss Lucy said. "You have too many familiars for the schooling to feel as natural as it once did. Plus, you were never one for learning through high school or college."

Tara shrugged. "I got good enough grades, but it really wasn't my thing." Unlike people like Kyle, who not only excelled at school but had actually enjoyed it.

"Exactly," Miss Lucy said. "You have power, my dear. You always did. It's always just been a matter of harnessing it. Directing it."

Tara didn't agree, but nodded anyway. Her problem with Miss Lucy had been much more fundamental: Miss Lucy and her coven weren't concerned with the betterment of others, but with more personal gain. And it showed—everyone in her coven was rich. Really, really rich.

While Tara and her coven were mostly poor. They worked actively to help those around them.

If there was some sort of catastrophe, Tara would want her crew around her, not any of Miss Lucy's.

"So will you join us?" Tara asked. "It won't do anyone any good if all of Portland gets destroyed. Along with most of the west coast."

"It won't work," Miss Lucy warned. "Whatever you have in mind. In the end, you won't be able to pull the trigger and eliminate the Riprap man."

Tara shook her head. "If it's his life versus millions of others, I think I'll be able to choose him."

Miss Lucy gave her a sly smile. "It doesn't matter. I choose to work with you anyway. I am interested in meeting the others I your coven. Particularly this Lucius."

Tara nodded, her heart saddened but she should have expected it.

Miss Lucy would never lie to her. She didn't always state her intent out loud, but Tara had gotten very good over the years at reading between the lines.

While Sheila might try to take over Tara's entire coven, Miss Lucy had merely set her sights on the strongest member of Tara's group. Lucius.

And while Tara knew that Lucius enjoyed working with her and the others, he had no loyalty. He wasn't human. He'd always assumed that he would use Tara while at the same time she would use him.

She'd lose him to Miss Lucy, once they met.

She was certain of it.

CHAPTER 3

The years have passed, and Portland herself is no longer the jewel she once was. I cannot stand the way that opportunities have been wasted by this local government of ours! At least the shanty towns have mostly been moved on as people leave the region. Portland is no longer growing, however. I miss the days when multiple bridges and projects were all going at the same time. I'm hopeful, however, that this conflict in Europe might bring more jobs to the region, as the last major war did. That perhaps our fine ports will be busy again. The great river god doesn't see the value of progress, doesn't understand how this stagnation will sour men's souls. I can only do so much to prod them on, however.

Wilson Evermore, Protector of Portland and Scourge of the Wasteful, 1939.

TARA GOT LUCIUS TO AGREE TO MEET WITH HER BEFORE the covens all descended on one another. They met in one of the parks just west of the city, where the trees met the water and great swaths of green grass filled the area. Though it was late, close to eight PM, it was still light out. Couples roamed the paths, as did parents pushing their SUV-sized strollers. The homeless were kept out of the park proper, and only took up one long edge, close to the street.

Tara still wouldn't want to go through this park at night. She could take care of herself, but she didn't want to have to.

Lucius strode up to the fountain she stood beside. He was carrying his cane that evening, an elegant black resin piece tipped on the bottom with silver. The top was in the form of a snake's head, a great cobra with the hood extended, also done in silver. Today he wore an impeccably tailored blue shirt that matched the intensity of his eyes, with cool gray pants.

"Good evening, my dear," Lucius said, giving her a frankly appraising look. "Don't tell me that you've finally decided to grant me my fondest wish of an intimate evening."

Tara snorted and rolled her eyes at him. She knew that Lucius was actually serious, and wanted to spend intimate time with her. She also couldn't even imagine what that would entail.

Lucius wasn't human. Anytime he let his mask slip, the alien nature of him made Tara's skin crawl. No matter how pretty the mask, she couldn't imagine getting closer.

"Then what task brings us together this evening?" Lucius said. His eyes practically twinkled at her as he grinned. "Perhaps some lovely magic, just the two of us?"

"No," Tara said, "I'd never even considered that, actually."

"Never thought about a *pas de duex*? Never?" Lucius said, teasing her. "You and Ginny do it all the time."

"We don't plan on performing magic together," Tara said. "It just happens."

"Your natural magic, yes, it ebbs and flows," Lucius said.

"Can you sense it?" Tara asked.

Lucius appeared to consider his reply. "In a way, yes. But only when I'm paying attention. Otherwise it will just flow past me like a soft, spring breeze. You don't pay attention to every spring breeze, do you?"

"No," Tara said. "But maybe I should." Ginny, after all, was really a wind witch, even though she'd developed something of an affinity toward water, now. Was part of their ability with each other because their winds interacted?

"So, no dancing, no magic, whatever are we to do?" Lucius asked. "Oh, wait. You don't want to do that either."

Tara sighed. "What I do want to do is to walk and talk with you for a bit," she said, starting down one of the paths.

Lucius caught up with her immediately. "Of course, my dear. What do you wish to discuss with me so far away from any of the others?"

"I've taken your advice," Tara said seriously. "I've asked both Miss Lucy and Sheila's coven to join with ours, to fight the Riprap man."

"Have you, now?" Lucius said. He sounded surprised. "I hadn't thought that you'd be able to share the power like that."

"I'm not sure how active I'll be in the group," Tara said.

"Do tell," Lucius said.

"We need to draw the attention of the Riprap man," Tara said seriously. "We can't just wait for another tremor, or bring the group together and hope that we get lucky enough to be able to find him."

"That's true," Lucius said. "So how do you plan on drawing him to you?"

"I will go out and challenge him," Tara said. "Someplace in the wilderness, where I would be more easily ambushed."

"You mean your physical presence? Not just a projected one?" Lucius said, his eyes wide. "I'm not sure I would recommend that."

"But it's the surest way to draw the Riprap man to us," Tara pointed out. "Mulinohana can't help us call him. Soot hasn't been able to find him, unless he wants to be found."

"It would be dangerous, you alone, out in the wild," Lucius said, turning serious for the first time that evening.

"I had hoped I wouldn't be completely alone," Tara said. Lucius was the most powerful being in her coven. She'd hoped that he would volunteer to help her confront the Riprap man.

"I see," Lucas said. He stopped walking, making Tara pause as well.

She felt her breath catch. Was this one bridge too far? Would Lucas not only say no, but leave the coven because she'd asked?

Lucas shook his head, sending Tara's heart plummeting. "No, I will not go with you."

Before Tara could say, maybe even apologize for asking, Lucas said, "Do you want me to call one of my brethren to help?"

Tara blinked, surprised by the offer. She'd never even

considered that Lucius might be able to bring in more help. "Would that be possible?" she said.

"Let me make some inquiries," Lucius said. "There are never many of my kind in any single location. We tend to be solitary. However, with a threat like this, they may be drawn in. If only for the novelty, if nothing else."

"What, of possibly saving the world?" Tara asked.

Lucius's laughter ran coldly down her spine. "Oh, no. That would never appeal to anyone I know. No, it's the chance to work with one of your kind."

"What do you mean?" Tara said, confused. Surely Lucius and the others had worked with humans before. Witches, even.

"Just leave it all up to me," Lucius said with a negligent wave of his hand as he strode away, leaving Tara far behind.

Tara wasn't certain if she should feel relieved that Lucius had a plan and wanted to help, or if she should be terrified that she actually had no idea what he was up to.

Or possibly a little of both.

WHILE KAEDE AND THE REST WANTED TO MEET AT Hallowed Ground, Miss Lucy as well as Sheila didn't want to. It would put them distinctly ill at ease, being in another coven's sacred spot.

It took some negotiations, but they finally all agreed to meet at the waterfront park, close to the river. They would meet twice. Once as a dress rehearsal, to make sure that the three groups could mesh their power together, then again the following night, when Tara would be far, far away in one of the state forests nearby Portland, trying to draw the Riprap man to her.

Lucius assured her that everything was all set, she just had to let him know when she was leaving the next day. It didn't make her feel any better that someone, or possibly just something, would be invisibly following her.

Still, it was better to have some sort of backup rather than none at all.

The group met at seven PM. Tara and her friends actually got to the park early for a cookout. They grilled hotdogs and ate baked beans, as well as a lovely green salad that Ginny provided. They found themselves laughing and giggling over nothing, as if the stress had just gotten too much and they found everything funny.

Kaede turned out to be able to do a killer imitation of Lucius, including not just his snide tone but all his mannerisms. Kyle showed them the new skill he'd picked up: juggling. And Richard regaled them with old stories of Portland, how the area had been settled, the stupid things that some of the original settlers had done.

Tara hadn't realized how much she missed this sort of comradery. She performed magic with these people, hung out with them afterwards, but rarely shared meals with them. Except for Kaede, as they tended to eat together every Sunday after they'd served the homeless.

"Thank you," Tara said, beaming at all of them as they started cleaning up.

"We all needed this," Kyle said. He nodded over her shoulder. "Incoming."

Tara turned to see Sheila walking at the head of her coven. She carried herself like a warrior going into battle.

In many ways, Tara could see her point.

Miss Lucy and her folks appeared at the same time on Tara's left. They carried themselves differently, more like landed gentry walking toward the croquet fields. They were obviously here to do Tara a favor, and possibly to enrich themseslves. Nothing more.

Nothing important, like possibly saving the city.

Tara sighed and shook her head. There wasn't anything she could say to either group. As part of the negotiations between the three groups, she'd agreed to only speak to Sheila and Miss Lucy, and not try to recruit anyone beyond them. The other two had promised the same, though the time for recruiting had been very precisely limited.

It was an unusual enough gathering, to bring three covens together this way. Having some rules in place would help smooth out some of the inevitable conflicts.

Miss Lucy had brought twenty-one with her, while Sheila had brought fifteen. Tara felt dwarfed by the mere six she had supporting her.

Yet, when she strode forward to meet with the other two witches, she felt the strength of her people flowing toward her.

They believed in her. They would trust her to do the right thing.

"Miss Lucy. Sheila," Tara said, greeting them. "Thank you for coming tonight."

"It was our pleasure, darling," Miss Lucy assured her.

"The city has need of us," Sheila said. "We came."

Tara realized that if they were successful, no matter who had actually done the work, Sheila and her coven would claim all the credit.

Fortunately, Tara didn't care about that. Nor did Miss Lucy.

"Tonight is the dry run," Tara told the two women. "We're here to fine tune how we work together. Tomorrow night we'll go and see if we can track down the Riprap man."

"I'm assuming you have a plan for that," Sheila said.

"Yes," Tara said. "It's why I'll help bring the groups together initially, but then I will step to the side and let Kaede take over the focus."

"We agreed to work with you," Miss Lucy said. Her voice took on a dark tone. "Not some other leader."

"And you are," Tara said. "But I need to leave, physically, and trap the Riprap man."

"You're using yourself as bait?" Sheila said, her eyes narrowing as if she hadn't considered how it would be done.

"I am," Tara told them.

Sheila appeared to consider this new twist for a moment. "Yes, that will do," she said, nodding.

Tara wasn't certain what Sheila meant, exactly, if she considered this an easy solution to the continuing problem that Tara presented.

"You can be sure that we'll maintain our efforts even without you here," Miss Lucy said, obviously challenging Sheila.

"Yes, we will," Sheila said.

Tara wasn't sure who was going to be the adult in this group when she stepped away. It probably wouldn't be either of these two.

"All right," Tara said. "The first step is to get everyone arranged in concentric circles around us."

"Have you ever worked with another coven before?" Miss Lucy asked. She seemed intrigued.

"No," Tara said. "But I've studied the theory."

"Theory?" Sheila said obviously surprised. "What theory?"

Tara smiled at them. "Old lore that I've discovered." She didn't bother to explain that Richard, her research librarian, had dug deep into old archives, doing many inter-library loans, and had found the most interesting books as a result.

There actually had been a small pamphlet published back in the 1960s that explained exactly how to mesh the powers of more than one coven together. It had obviously been some handout for another group. She had no idea if it actually worked. But she intended to find out tonight.

Both Miss Lucy and Sheila were taken aback by Tara's assurance that she already had a plan, and that it came from old lore. Tara wondered if both of them had just assumed that they'd be the leader of the meshed coven, and not her and her group.

They ended up with three circles of witches loosely circled around the inner group of Tara, Sheila, and Miss Lucy. Tara faced the river, while the other two faced the city. Tara arranged the groups so that the strongest witches were closer in, and the less powerful one further out. Richard was in the outermost circle, while Kaede and Lucius were in the inner most. Both Ginny and Kyle were in the middle ring.

"It's important to stay in your place," Tara warned, speaking loudly enough so that everyone could hear her. "The circles have to be maintained."

The pamphlet had only had a single sentence warning about it, how the magic would explode outward it if wasn't properly contained by the circles, then drained away.

Finally, they were ready to begin. Kaede stood directly behind Tara, ready to trade places with her once the groups had all been joined.

Tara started off the prayers, asking for Brigid and Sammil to guide them. Sheila took up the next part, asking the winds to carry their prayers to all who needed to hear them. Then Miss Lucy spoke, asking the guardians of their souls and the protectors of the dead to watch over them.

Power suddenly started flowing between the three of them. It wasn't the warm strong power that she was used to with her coven. Instead, it was a much colder power, sleek even. It slid around them, instead of buoying her up. She thought of it as a blue ribbon that tied them together, as opposed to the warm, golden light that seemed to infuse her coven normally.

That ribbon was useful, though. Tara took the image in her mind and passed it back to the second circle, standing around them. She felt the power of the two groups as they got tied together. It was heady, standing on a wave of strength.

Why didn't witches come together more often to do this sort of thing? There must be a cost that Tara wasn't aware of. They could do so much good work this way!

Tara saw her mistake as she brought in the next group, tying them into the first two circles. Despite how powerful Miss Lucy, Sheila, and Tara were, controlling this much power was going to take tremendous effort.

Tara let the groups hum along for a few moments, trying to modulate the strength of the groups. There had to be a way of narrowing the firehose coming at her. She realized that all the hair on the back of her neck was now standing, as was the hair along her arms. The smell of burnt grass lay heavy on the air. Her stomach churned, her entire body unhappy with all the foreign magic flowing through her.

Tara looked at the other two women to see how they were holding up. Miss Lucy had her eyes closed and a grimace on her face. She was obviously straining as well to keep up with everything pouring into the three of them.

Sheila had her eyes open, but was staring off into space, not seeing anything that was in front of her. She panted slightly, as if she was walking quickly down the sidewalk. Tara could still feel where the flow of energy was off in the woman, how only one of her feet connected firmly to the ground.

Should Tara bring up the third circle of power? While they would be the weakest of the three, it would still mean adding more to an already creaking structure.

Was there a way of just adding a part of it? No. Each circle was a complete entity. She would have to add all of it, or none of it.

Tara tried to move slowly, very slowly, seeking to just allow the last circle's power to seep into what they already had. She found herself shaking with the effort. It was like trying to hold back a stampeding horse. Her arms trembled. Her legs grew shaky as well.

No. Wait.

She wasn't shaking.

The ground was.

Tara clung to the hands of the other witches. Had the Riprap man come to attack them?

A new presence lurked underground, directly beneath their feet. It would overwhelm them shortly.

Tara forced her attention *down*, into the earth, to try to stop whatever was there.

It surprised her when instead of staying in the cold, dank earth, she found herself in an open space, a room carved out of the rock. She was surrounded by a group of women, all holding hands. They chanted, channeling their power at her. They weren't chanting in English but used what sounded to Tara like nonsense syllables.

Tara tried to push back at the waves of magic washing over her, but it was like trying to stop the heat of a fire by merely waving your hands. The women were intent on… something. Helping her? Destroying her?

It took Tara a few moments to realize that this new

coven was composed of the souls of all the witches who the Riprap man had killed and then bound to the bridges across the Willamette river. Dorothy Parkerson stood in front of her, still dressed stylishly in a maroon sweater and skirt, with dark curls drawn back into a poodle cut and a heart-shaped face.

However, like all the women, only the whites of her eyes showed. She looked like a woman possessed.

What were they doing? Why had they gathered? Why were they trying to overwhelm Tara and the connected covens?

"Stop!" Tara said. Or at least tried to say. The strength of their call was drowning her.

The ground trembled again, a tremor passing through the room like a cold wave.

Tara pushed her soul back up above the ground, rejoining her body. Both Sheila and Miss Lucy now looked at her, as if demanding answers that she couldn't give them.

Were the tremors real? Or was she just feeling them on the cosmic plane?

A scream filled the air. The power of the group suddenly spiraled out of control. Tara felt her focus release. The magic snapped loose, sparking like a powerline. That cool ribbon of power now jerked around the circles, shocking individuals when it touched them.

Tara turned to see the Riprap man advancing on them. He'd forced his way into the third circle, forcing two of the witches apart, breaking the circle, making them drop their hands.

He had his hands on the wrists of two of the individuals in the middle circle. Though his bare torso was made of stone, he still appeared to be struggling to make the witches let go of each other's hands.

What held them together wasn't their physical strength but the magical power flowing around the circle.

Tara had planned on an orderly releasing of the circles and the individuals. However, they'd all be damaged further if the Riprap man just broke them apart. She tried to untie the circles from where they'd been joined. The third circle had been torn loose.

She almost got the blue ribbons of power disconnected when the Riprap man forced the two witches apart.

Again, the backlash of power nearly knocked Tara from her feet. She stubbornly held on, gritting her teeth. She shook her head, trying to focus. She must untie the next circle before the Riprap man tore it apart.

The witches from the bridges kept pouring out their strength, distracting her from being able to do the work in front of her. Was that why they'd gathered? To act as a distraction? It had worked. She could barely see what was in front of her. The sound of their chanting suddenly filled her ears, along with the roaring of the ocean.

The blue ribbon of power had grown blazing hot. She still grabbed hold of it with both hands and tugged at the knot, drawing it apart.

A new power slid in beside her. Tara's first instinct was to push it away, snarling. It took her a moment to realize that Lucius was trying to help. She gratefully relinquished some of her control. He smoothly stepped in and untied the two groups before the Riprap man could finish his attack.

As the individuals in the group stepped away, back from each other, dazed, the Riprap man caught Tara's eye.

I'm coming for you next he told her clearly before he disappeared.

Tara shook her head and let go of Miss Lucy and Sheila's hands. They looked at each other, clearly shocked and stunned.

What had just happened?

The chanting from the coven working underneath them faded away as everyone came slowly to their senses.

Someone touched Tara on the shoulder. She turned to see Kaede pointing at someone who'd fallen to the ground.

Tara raced over to where Richard had fallen. He was still out cold, his skin waxy and pale. One of the other coven members held onto his wrist in a professional manner, obviously measuring his pulse.

"Heartbeat is rapid but slowing," the woman said. "He had a big shock."

"What in the hell were you doing bringing a mundane into the circle?" someone else demanded, a person Tara didn't know.

"He knew the risk," Tara said wearily. She pushed Richard's hair back from his forehead. "Come on. Come on back to me."

"Obviously, he didn't," Sheila said, coming up to stand behind Tara. "None of us did."

Tara hung her head. Sheila was right. None of them had ever tried anything like this before. And no one had had any idea of how it actually worked.

"Maybe with a smaller group—" Tara started to say.

"No," Miss Lucy said firmly. "I am not risking any more of my people."

Tara sat back on her heels and wearily watched Sheila and Miss Lucy gather their covens back together. She could never ask either of them for help, not ever again.

The amount of power that had poured through Tara and the others had been spectacular to behold.

It had also been far too much for any of them. Perhaps if they'd brought together two groups that had several level six witches as the leads, then backed the with much weaker witches, it would have worked. But the power levels were always going to be tricky.

"Ye didn't have a bad idea," Ginny said, coming up quietly. She sank down next to Tara, then reached out and held her hand. "We just needed more time."

Tara nodded. Time they didn't have, would never have. If she ever tried to bring together such a group again, the Riprap man would be there, sure to tear it apart.

Richard finally blinked open his eyes. Color hadn't returned to his face, but at least he was awake. "What… what happened?"

Surprisingly, Lucius was the one who responded. "A very interesting amalgamation of events," he said. "I suggest that tonight, we all rest. Then we should gather tomorrow night, as we had planned."

"Why?" Kyle asked. "We aren't still going after the Riprap man, are we?"

Lucius gave him an enigmatic smile. "I'll see you at Hallowed Ground," he said before he turned and walked away.

"Do you think he has a plan?" Ginny asked Tara.

"I sure hope so," Tara said. "Because I'm all out of ideas."

CHAPTER 4

More immigrants continue to pour into the city. Fortunately, they are all segregated into Vanport, on the border between Washington and Oregon, a little east of Portland. It's a bustling place, a city open twenty-four hours a day as mighty ships are built. I revel in the growth of fair shining Portland, the city expanding as it should. I wouldn't wish this war to go on forever, as I've seen the devastated men who've returned, the limbless or blind few. Still, I cannot help but hope that it lasts many more years as the city continues to outshine itself.

Wilson Evermore, Former Engineer and Hunter of Witches, 1942

TARA WOKE THE NEXT MORNING, FEELING AS THOUGH NOT just her body but her soul was bruised as well. She groaned as she stretched, resenting her alarm clock, the fact that she had to make a living and couldn't just call in sick to work, the realization that she was going to have to push herself all day just to make it through.

Teruko still lay beside her. He'd taken on a much larger form that night, so he could heat up her entire back. She was grateful to him, and his shared warmth, particularly how he'd purred and tried to comfort her.

Soot had even yielded his place on the bed to give Tara and Teruko more room, though he now poked his head up and looked hopefully at her. Though he was really an imbodied wind, and he didn't really need walks, he still needed to spend time with her on a regular basis, generally playing and chasing after things for her.

Tara did not want to move. Did not want to try to force herself up. She still made herself sit up on the bed, groaning again as she moved.

Outside, light shone against the blinds. At least it was going to be another sunny day, though rain was predicted for later that week. Tara stretched out to touch her toes, fighting off the wave of dizziness that overtook her.

She just needed some food. Then she'd be fine.

Her little room in the house that she shared with four other people still felt cozy to her. She didn't need a lot—just space for a small fridge where she could keep herbs and her own plants, the big bed in the center that she shared with her familiars, a dresser for her clothes and a desk where she could study. She had the rest of the house where she could go and hang out with the others if she wanted to, as well as a shared kitchen and the large backyard. She was only a few blocks away from the river. She could smell the water every time she stepped outside.

Tara gave Teruko a few more skirtches under the chin, ignoring his meow of protest when she finally pushed herself off the bed. She listed to one side. Wow. She hadn't expected to feel so dizzy. It was as if her inner ear was off balance.

That made sense, actually, given the way that the evening had gone. The great lashes of power that the group had undergone had roughed up all of her insides. It was as though her body, the container for herself, had been forcibly held still, while all of her insides had been vigorously shaken.

She just couldn't take the day off from the Y, though. She didn't have any more vacation days available, not unless she didn't take off time when the summer solstice came in a few weeks. And that wouldn't be right.

Tara pushed herself through her morning, walking with Soot to the MAX stop, throwing a ball that he could chase and bring back to her as they made their way along the few blocks. The day was already warm, and Tara was cursing her decision to wear jeans and not shorts that morning. She passed by a new encampment of homeless close to the stop. They were transient, wouldn't stay, she felt certain. Since she'd been working at Hallowed Ground, she'd become a much better judge of the various stages of homelessness.

It had made sense to her that Hallowed Ground focused on prevention, rather than just on taking care of people in the street. It was so much harder to get out of the cycle once you'd started down that path.

There wasn't anything she could do for this group of kids, however. They were pretty used to the street, had probably been there a few years. They would hold each other back if one of them tried to break out and leave. Groups like that needed to be rescued all at once, if at all.

Tara sank gratefully into a seat on the train when it arrived. It was still before seven, and many of the commuters had already gotten off downtown, before the train arrived in her neighborhood.

Though Tara found her body as well as her thoughts still moving slowly, she found herself circling back to what had happened the night before, thinking about the coven of witches who lived under the bridges, and finding herself comparing them to the posse of homeless kids she'd just passed.

What was the connection? Were they similar, in that if one of the witches tried to leave, the others would all hold her back? How did they depend on each other?

Tara had never forgotten going down to visit Dorothy. She and the others in the coven had discussed whether or not it would be possible to free those souls. However, the question had always come back to whether or not the witches would want to be freed. Yes, they were tied to their location, or as Dorothy had called, *cell sweet cell.*

But if they were freed, would they die? Probably. And that was the biggest problem. Did they want to die? To pass on? Or did they prefer their current existence, even if they were tied to a single place and unable to move around much?

Tara just didn't know. She wasn't sure if she wanted to try to visit them to ask, particularly after last night. Would they just attack her again?

Why had they attacked? Had it been them attacking? Or had the Riprap man somehow forced them into it? They hadn't seemed normal or right, with their eyes all rolled back in their heads. Had they been trying to help? It had been too much power coming at Tara all at once.

Somehow, Tara was going to have to communicate with that coven. Because she was *persona non gratis* with the living covens she had a connection to in Portland at this point.

Tara wasn't sure how she made it through the day. She rested when she could between classes, even going so far as to catch a quick catnap in the breakroom when she was supposedly eating her lunch. There wasn't enough caffeine in the world to wake her up, though she drank black tea all throughout the day.

She didn't have time to go home after she finished teaching swimming at the Y—instead she caught a bus directly to Hallowed Ground. The solid building still appeared to be a sanctuary to her as she walked up. The walls were a white stucco, and looked freshly painted, though Tara knew that was just a spell that Kaede had put up.

Tara entered through the back, heading directly to the industrial kitchen. Alaska was there, preparing herself a snack. She'd been doing peacock colored hair recently, with dark green and blue highlights. She still had what appeared to be the requisite number of piercings on her face, through her ears, as well as a few exotic ones, like the bars across her collar bone. Today she wore what Tara would call modern grunge—a yellow and black flannel shirt covered over in patches, as well as black jeans with holes in them.

"You look as bad as Kaede," the younger woman said as soon as she saw Tara. Despite how tough and world weary Alaska tried to sound, she always gave Tara the impression of being bird-brittle.

"Thanks," Tara said, not bothering to hide her sarcasm. She yawned. "Sorry. Can't help it."

"How bad is it this time?" Alaska asked quietly as Tara pulled out tea supplies and put them on one of the carts, getting ready for her "teashop."

"Bad," Tara admitted. They still had no idea how they were going to stop the Riprap man.

"Do we need to call in the troops?" Alaska said. "Like we did last time?"

"No," Tara said with a shudder. "We tried that last night. Didn't work."

"Wasn't really your people," Alaska replied, her chin raising in defiance. "You should trust us instead."

"It isn't that," Tara said. "I just—we don't want you hurt."

Richard had checked in with Tara midmorning. Ginny had stayed with him overnight. He was finally recovering, though he said his insides were still spinning. He insisted that he was going to come see them that night, though he was planning on sleeping all day long.

How badly could it all have gone if there had been a large group of mundanes involved instead?

"We can take care of our own," Alaska said hotly.

"I know you can," Tara said. "And believe me, I'm grateful for all the help you can give. We all are. This is just…different."

"And bad," Alaska said.

Tara nodded. "And bad." She paused, then added, "If we can figure out a way of using you without killing you all, we will call on you."

Alaska blinked at her, looking surprised. "You're serious."

Tara nodded and shook her head, trying to prevent another yawn. "I am. Death awaits us. Hopefully only if we fail, and not necessarily if we succeed also."

That appeared to mollify Alaska some and she merely nodded as Tara left the kitchen with her full cart.

Someone else had already set up the table in the corner for Tara to work at, for which she was incredibly grateful.

Three lines of tables had been set up across the back of the room, where a few different groups of teens diligently worked at their homework. Storytime was taking place in the far corner, with a group of younger kids enthralled by Sonja and her current yarn.

Tara slowly moved her tea carriers to the table, along with her tea kettle. The two large jugs for water were already filled and waiting for her.

After Tara slid the cart to the side, and let herself sit heavily on the stool thoughtfully provided, her first customers came up. They were fraternal twins, not identical. Tara guessed that they were both between seven and eight. The boy, DeAndre, wore his hair shaved close to his head with a cute half-moon pattern carved into at the front. The girl, DeLilah, wore her hair in a looser braid, though Tara had heard her threaten to just shave her head once she was older. They both had the usual T-shirts and jeans on, and at least looked as though they were eating enough finally.

"What can I do for you?" Tara said smiling at them. Though they weren't identical twins, they still shared some of that "twinness" that she'd only heard about. They frequently appeared to talk with each other without saying a word out loud.

They shared a look, then DeAndre took a half step forward, obviously intending on speaking for the pair of them today. "We need something to help us with math," he said seriously.

"Tell me more," Tara said.

DeAndre looked again at his sister before he continued. "I'm not as good at math as DeLilah," he said after a moment.

"Is there a problem with the numbers?" Tara knew to ask. "Do they dance around on the page?"

DeAndre looked horrified at her. "No! Why would they do that?"

"That's what some people see," Tara clarified. "The numbers reverse themselves." She needed to make sure that this wasn't some sort of dyslexia that the boy had.

"No. It's just they don't make come as easily to me as they do to her," DeAndre said, jerking his thumb in the direction of his sister. "And they should." He paused, then added, "I'm the boy. I'm supposed to be good at math."

Tara suddenly understood the problem. It wasn't that DeAndre was bad at math, she'd bet. It was that his sister was better.

And girls weren't supposed to be good at math. Everyone knew that.

"What if I tell you that some of the most famous mathematicians in the world were women?" Tara said.

DeAndre scowled at her. Tara snuck a quick peek at DeLilah. She was beaming. Tara could practically hear her singsong voice saying, "I told you so."

"It's okay if your sister is better at math than you are," Tara added.

DeAndre just shook his head no. That wasn't the way the world worked, at least according to him, as well as whoever he'd been listening to.

"What can DeAndre do better than you?" Tara said, asking DeLilah.

"Lots of things!" the little girl enthused. "He's a really good runner. And he can hit a ball harder than I can."

"How about in school?" Tara said, knowing that she might be getting into sticky territory here.

"He's really good at drawing," DeLilah said.

DeAndre just scowled harder.

"Everyone says so," DeLilah added. "You can draw just about anything you see."

"But what good is that?" DeAndre said.

Tara knew better than to try to convince him that he could do art someday. He wouldn't see the value in that. "You know the games you see some of the older kids playing on their phones?"

DeAndre nodded warily.

"Someone has to draw those characters, you know," she said. "You could become a famous video game designer someday."

"I don't need math for that?" DeAndre said, still suspicious.

"Maybe a little," Tara said, as she really didn't know. "However, just because your sister is better at math doesn't mean you're not any good. Right?"

"She's still better," DeAndre said, crossing his arms over his chest.

"What if I make you some tea to help you be a little bit better?" Tara said, not speaking the full truth. She didn't have anything that would actually make DeAndre better at a specific subject in school. What she did have was a tea that would help him be more accepting of who he was, who his sister was destined to be.

DeAndre nodded, finally feeling better that Tara might be able to provide some help. "And I'll give you a tea as well," Tara said, turning to DeLiliah, "that will help you run a little faster."

"I'd like that," the little girl said with a big grin.

Tara made her first tea for DeAndre, adding hyssop, licorice root, ginger, then some hibiscus to brighten up the flavor, as well as some honey. Though she'd felt depleted all day, she felt her magic finally stir itself, and send a tendril of something into the cup. It would calm the boy, and help him in their current situation.

For DeLiliah, Tara mixed together borage for courage,

as well as lemon balm and bee balm for quickness, not just of her body but of her mind as well, sweetened with some mint and honey.

The pair of them thanked her for their tea, promising to finish their homework early every night that week for payment so that they could help out more around the shelter.

Tara quickly fell into the rhythm of making tea, stirring in kindness and whatever else her clients needed. It was a very pleasant way to spend the afternoon. Mainly she listened, as that was what most of the kids needed—an adult who would listen to them and not immediately try to fix everything, not unless they specifically asked her to.

They didn't serve a full meal that night, opening up the doors and letting all the clients in. Instead, it was more of a family affair, the food all served family style—hamburgers, hotdogs, green salad and a red jello dessert. Kaede joined them, sharing a tired smile with Tara.

After they cleaned up, all the clients left and the rest of the coven began to show up. Ginny actually came early that night—possibly only the second or third time ever. She looked as pale and wan as Tara felt, the freckles standing out sharply across her nose and cheeks. At least her eyes didn't appear to be haunted, and she gave Tara a fierce hug when she came in.

The other arrived shortly. Richard looked like a dead man walking. Even Lucius had a bit of dark circles under his eyes, though to a lesser extent than everyone else.

Tara didn't call everyone into a circle that evening. She didn't think they'd have the power between them to stay standing. Instead, she served them all a warming tea, made from lavender, peppermint, and lemon balm, with more honey than she usually served.

They did all end up sitting in a circle anyway, pulling chairs out to the center of the room.

"Well, we sure did get our asses handed to us last night," Kyle started out with. He sounded sour, and his dark skin seemed pale that evening.

"I didn't expect the Riprap man to come and attack us that way," Tara said, feeling as though she needed to explain herself. Most of his attacks previously had been on more of an astral plane, rather than a physical one.

"No one did," Kaede said. "But we should never make that assumption again. He has a physical form. And he's coming for us. All of us, this time, no matter how his attention appears to be focused on Tara."

Tara nodded. She had to agree. The Riprap man no longer held anyone, or anything, sacred.

"What called him there, do ye think?" Ginny asked. "Was it all that power?"

"Maybe," Tara said. "Maybe not. I wonder if he was preparing for us already." She explained seeing the other coven when she'd gone underground, how they appeared to have been under his control. Though she was just guessing.

Lucius nodded. "I think they were under his power," he said after a moment. His melodic voice sounded much rougher than usual, hoarse and strained. "I think he was in the process of coming after us, or using that coven's power for some ill deed, when we interrupted him and his plans."

"But what was he trying to do?" Richard asked. "And has he used their power in the past?"

"Someone is going to have to go and talk with them again," Kyle said grimly.

Tara shuddered. She did *not* want to have to do that again. The first time she'd managed it using a potion that

Miss Lucy had concocted for her. It had been awful. She felt bile rising just thinking about it.

"Maybe not," Lucius said. "I think I have a plan that might work instead."

"Really?" Tara said, gratefulness overwhelming her.

"I had not anticipated that the Riprap man had such a physical presence anymore," Lucius stated. "I had believed that his presence is merely astral or mental at this time. But he still has a body. He just rarely uses it. And that can be used against him."

"Really? How? Tell us!"

Tara just sat still, thinking hard. She had never really considered that the Riprap man had both a physical as well as mental presence, and what that might mean.

"So you think that we can get at his body?" Tara asked finally, staring hard at Lucius. "Where do you think it is?"

She doubted that he was walking around in his physical body very often. In fact, she wasn't sure she'd ever actually seen him in the flesh, as it were. She might have only seen projections of him.

"Where was the first earthquake, that he blamed you for?" Lucius asked.

"Basically, out in the middle of nowhere," Tara said. "East of Portland."

"That's where we'll find him," Lucius said. "He struck as close to home as he could that first time. Now, he's branching out. I would bet he can't travel too far from it."

"I'd wondered, when he'd first started coming after me, if I could leave. Go to Wisconsin or someplace. If that would be out of his range," Tara said.

"I believe it would be, yes," Lucius said. "I consulted with a friend last night. He's game to go after the creature, in particular, his physical body, to help us."

"Do I still have to physically travel to there as well?"

Tara asked.

"All will be made clear soon," Lucius said.

A knock suddenly sounded on the door.

"Kaede, can you let our guest in?" Lucius asked.

Kaede shook zir head, but stood up slowly. "Are you sure about this?" ze asked.

"It would be rude of him to do aught but what we ask," Lucius assured zir.

"And you can get him to leave?" Kaede persisted, not heading toward the door yet.

"Trust me, he isn't interested in you or your kind," Lucius said.

Kaede shook zir head, but slowly moved toward the door. "I will hunt you down and make your bones sing for their supper if any harm comes to me or mine," ze warned before ze opened the door.

"You may enter, but only for this evening," Kaede told the individual who stood patiently outside.

"But of course," came the smooth reply.

The voice reminded Tara of Lucius. The being who stepped into the room bore a superficial resemblance to him as well. They were both tall, arrogant looking men with piercing blue eyes. While Lucius's hair was silver, this person's hair was jet black. They shared the same hawk nose and dimpled chin, and perhaps the same tailor, as they both wore beautiful handmade shirts and trousers that were impeccably fitted.

However, the similarities were just skin deep. No matter how alien Lucius might seem when he allowed his mask to slip, he had a life and vitality to him.

This person, this creature, did not. Instead of exuding life, he drained it.

If Lucius and his kind had inspired myths of elves and other horrible but bright creatures, the one who had just entered would have inspired myths of vampires and their deadly, life-sucking kin.

Tara found herself rising to her feet automatically. Soot appeared at her side, growling. Teruko showed up on her other side, spitting and hissing.

"Now, is that anyway to greet an invited guest?" Lucius scolding, standing and walking over to his guest. "Hello, Martin," he said, sticking out his hand.

"Hello, Lucius," Martin said. He had the same smooth, sardonic quality to his voice that Lucius had. "So it this your little group?"

Tara was surprised at the beam of pride that Lucius gave. "It is," he said simply. "And we are asking your help."

"Read me in," Martin said. He effortlessly snagged a chair and floated over to where the rest of the group still sat.

Tara glanced at Kaede, who nodded and warily sat down herself. Tara couldn't get either Soot or Teruko to leave, however, she did manage to get Soot to lay down next to her, while Teruko leaped onto her lap and settled down there, still giving Martin the occasional baleful stare.

"Martin, as you may have guessed, is possibly better equipped for dealing with the physical Riprap man than the rest of us," Lucius stated.

Tara nodded. She could see that. This…soul stealer, could possibly do the trick, and be able to handle the Riprap man better than any of them.

Miss Lucy had told Tara that in the end, she wasn't hard enough to deal with the Riprap man on her own. Her former mentor may have been right.

So Tara waited with the rest as Lucius and Kaede explained their problem, waiting to hear Martin's solution, hoping that it would solve all their ills.

CHAPTER 5

AFTER THE GROUP HAD DEVELOPED THEIR PLAN AND Martin had left, Kaede turned on Lucius. "Don't you ever, *ever*, invite someone like that here again," ze warned.

Lucius merely cocked one eyebrow at zir. "What,

someone who could save our souls and help us destroy the thing that is intent on destroying the city?"

"You know what I mean," Kaede said. Ze closed zir eyes and bent zir head in prayer for a moment.

Tara felt power rock through the room, as if all the protection sigils deep under the foundation of the building just lit up.

Even Lucius appeared impressed by the display.

"Never again," Kaede warned before ze stalked off.

"I didn't know ze would feel that strongly about it," Lucius offered into the awkward silence.

"What is Martin?" Richard asked. Of course he would. He was a research librarian. Though they'd all been alternately scared as well as repulsed by Martin's presence, only Richard would be the one who would like to learn more.

"He doesn't suck blood or some such nonsense," Lucius assured them. "He doesn't really take souls or energy, either. He's much more attracted to lay lines, the natural power girds of the land."

"Interesting," Richard said. "How does he—"

"While Martin is a dear old friend, I don't know much more than that," Lucius stated, holding off Richard's questions. "It isn't any of my business. I suggest you ask him yourself the next time you see him."

"Which would be never, right?" Kyle asked. "There's no reason for him to come visiting any of us at night."

"True," Lucius said, sounding reluctant. "But if you really want to meet with him again, let me know," he added, nodding to Richard.

After the rest had left, it was only Ginny and Tara still standing on the sidewalk outside Hallowed Ground, chatting.

"Will it work?" Ginny asked, sounding much more timid than Tara had ever heard the other witch before.

Tara had to shrug. "Lucius and Martin seem to think it will." The plan did have a certain elegance to it, she had to admit. Instead of trying to ambush the Riprap man with the combined strength of three covens, they'd go the physical route instead, and have Martin ready to grab him. Just their coven would be involved, ready to distract any non-physical projections of the Riprap man.

The plan still involved using Tara as bait. That part hadn't changed. And Lucius had hinted that there would be yet another being involved who would be following Tara.

"I don't know about any of this," Ginny said. "I don't like the idea of going out and hunting someone. Even the Riprap man."

They started walking along the sidewalk, heading back toward the MAX station. The night was calm and soft. Tara still felt exhausted and unsettled from the night before, and the talk and planning that evening made her feel older still. Her bones creaked as she walked, her knees protesting every step.

"I also don't feel great about the plan either," Tara said. "But I don't see how else we can get the Riprap man to stop. We can't negotiate with him. There's nothing he holds dear that we could use to threaten him. He used to care greatly for Portland. Now, he's turned his back on his city."

"Wouldn't it be better to bind him?" Ginny asked.

Tara had thought about that as well, more than once. "It would be," Tara agreed. "But I don't want to bind him to myself, personally, to turn him into some other sort of familiar. I'm not sure I can, that I'm strong enough, and I think that's just putting the problem off to another day. Once I passed, he's become a problem again."

"Ah," Ginny said. She still seemed thoughtful. "I just don't feel good about gunning for his soul."

"I don't either," Tara admitted. "But I haven't come up with any other solution."

Ginny reached out and touched Tara's arm. "I know ye don't have the time," she said. "But ye got to keep trying other paths. Other ways. Not ending another soul like this."

"I will try," Tara promised. Besides, if this didn't work, they'd be forced to find another way regardless.

"Thank you," Ginny said. She strode off then, calling her winds to her with a sharp whistle. A mass of dogs appeared around her, like a dogwalker with a dozen clients.

Tara made her way to the MAX station with her own wind trotting beside her. She had the same misgivings at Ginny. However, they had run out of options.

The Riprap man was coming for them all. And she had to stop him. Even if it meant destroying his soul.

Tara slept heavy and deep that night. Her body seemed happier for the rest. She didn't have to work at the Y that day, having already changed shifts with someone else. Instead, today she was going up into the hills.

Far up into the hills.

She packed herself a hearty lunch, as well as made a large thermos of tea to share. Martin appeared in a Jeep promptly at nine AM, as promised. It was painted brown and covered in mud, as if he'd just driven it off from some dirt road. The vehicle didn't really have doors, just a front windshield and a rag top. It rode high on its knobby wheels and looked as though it could roll over just about anything.

Martin himself was dressed more like a quaint Englishman on safari, with a beige safari jacket with many pockets and wide brimmed hat. He also wore shorts, tall white socks, and black leather hiking boots.

However, the grin he gave her was that of a shark's. He seemed ready for a good hunt.

Fortunately, so was she.

They headed out of town, Martin unerringly finding the quickest route. It impressed Tara, as she'd assumed they'd be stuck in morning rush-hour traffic for a good hour. He quickly made his way east, up into the hills there.

Tara found that Martin was staring at her as he drove. It wasn't easy to talk in the Jeep. The sound of wind kept conversation to a minimum. But once they left the freeway and were heading more slowly along a winding, two-lane road, Martin asked her, "How did you meet Lucius?"

"He was introduced to me," Tara said. "A friend of a friend." Which was true enough. She didn't want to bring Kyle into the picture. She still was unsure what their current relationship was.

But Martin just nodded. "That was how I met him as well. Years and years ago. A friend of a friend. It surprised me when I found out he was working with you lot."

Tara shrugged. Lucius had only offered to stay with them for a while. She assumed that sooner or later he'd get bored and move on. She was almost surprised that he hadn't so far. It had almost been a year, now.

"He assures me that your group is something quite special," Martin continued.

Tara just smiled at him. Obviously, Martin was looking for information. Tara wasn't sure what he wanted. Eventually she replied. "I think our group is special as well," she said. "We have a range of abilities, not just a hierarchy, like a regular coven."

"I noticed that," Martin said. "I approve. I think that blended families work best."

"Blended families?" Tara asked.

"Yes. Your coven is like a family unit, as I understand them, correct?" Martin said.

"Yes, a family of choice," Tara said.

"I like that term," Martin said. "There's no such thing as a blended family for us," he said, sounding sad.

"Why is that?" Tara said, mainly because she felt he was expecting some sort of response.

"Well…my kind doesn't eat people. Not really. Not like your myths of vampires," Martin said. "But we do wear them down, eventually." He shrugged. "Just our nature, I suppose."

Tara nodded. She could see how that might be. Even just spending an hour or so with Martin had brought her exhaustion back to the forefront. She couldn't imagine what it would be like to actually have to live with such a creature.

They traveled a bit more up the two lane road until Martin told Tara, "Hang on."

She reached for the strap hanging off the roll bar as he made a sharp turn up a forest service road. He didn't bother to slow down at all once they did, instead, bouncing hard along the rutted gravel. Trees surrounded them. The smell of sunbaked wood and fresh pine rolled over her. Thick bushes grew under the canopy of trees. She saw tiny animals race off the road as they approached. All she heard was the racing of the engine, now.

Tara kept hold of the strap as they sped under the trees. She wasn't sure what the hurry was. They had most of the day ahead of them, until the coven met later that evening.

Martin had changed as soon as they'd gotten off the

road. His eyes grew intent as he drove, and the look he gave when he glanced her way chilled her very soul.

This was the hunter that Lucius had described.

Martin branched off the service road onto something not much more than an improved animal track. It still had ruts from a car, but it was greatly overgrown with tall grass that whipped past them. They crossed into brilliant sunlight, then back under the trees again.

Tara had the impression that they were climbing again, albeit slowly. It wasn't until Martin pulled into a clearing and slammed the brakes on that she realized just how high they'd gotten.

Ahead of her spread a vast panorama. Trees filled the valley below. Birds flew above the greenery. Steep yellow and gray cliffs led down, boulders peeking out from under the grass. Far below, Tara sensed water, a small river, compared to what had once been a mighty flow.

The silence seemed deafening at first. Tara still felt herself rocking, as if the car still had forward momentum.

She looked over at Martin. He nodded at her. "We're here," he announced. He stood up, bending himself over the front roll bar to look down and around. "And he knows it."

WHILE MARTIN SEEMED TO HAVE AN UNNATURAL ABILITY to descend along the rough animal track at the head of the cliff, Tara had to take her time, placing her boots carefully along the trail, making sure that she didn't either twist her ankle or fall to her death.

Fortunately, they didn't have to make it all the way to the bottom of the chasm. If they had, she would have insisted that they bring camping gear or something. As it was, she really wasn't looking forward to having to make it up that track after some sort of fight.

Martin led them to a wide meadow about halfway down the cliff that Tara hadn't seen from the top. It seemed like such a beautiful, peaceful place. The sun shone down on them cheerfully. Little white flowers danced at the ends of tall stalks. Tiny blue butterflies flew across the tops of them. The air smelled of rocks baked by the warm sunlight. The meadow itself was maybe about twenty feet across, ten wide. The back of was delaminated by the cliff face, just as the front was as well.

Tara would have loved to have stayed here. Maybe with a picnic or something.

Except for one thing.

The whitish boulders that she saw piled haphazardly roughly in the center of the meadow started moving.

The Riprap man rose, staring ominously at them.

Crap.

Tara and Martin weren't supposed to find him until later that evening, after the coven had gathered in Hallowed Ground.

Too late now.

TARA HAD A LITTLE DEFENSIVE MAGIC, MERELY A SORT OF bubble shield that she called up around herself. As for attacking, she knew that as long as she stayed in control of her familiars, they could do a lot of damage. However, she was afraid to send them into the fight. The Riprap man could easily wrest Soot and Teruko's loyalty from Tara, getting them to attack Martin instead.

At the moment, none of them needed to do much. The Riprap man and Martin circled each other. Tara found it difficult to watch, as neither of them had much of a human aspect anymore. Instead, it was like watching two monsters who were all too real face off.

Martin had grown white and pale, like a slug who lived underground. He'd also grown more slender and willowy, appearing as a living whip. He moved slowly as he faced off with his opponent, circling to the right, then to the left.

The Riprap man's physical body resembled the one Tara had always seen, made out of hard stone. Only this stone was eroded and rough. His face was obscured by the rock, his expression fixed in rage. Instead of deep blue, his eyes were now pits of darkness. He wore no trousers, not that he needed any, as he had nothing remaining of his gender.

The Riprap man roared his displeasure at Martin instead of taunting him with words. Tara wondered if he'd actually lost all language when he took on stone form, or at least the ability to form speech, given how frozen all of him now seemed. Martin hissed in return, like an overgrown snake. The sound chilled Tara to the quick, reminding her once again that she faced nothing human.

She still hesitated to send either Soot or Teruko forward, afraid she might distract Martin and not the Riprap man.

Suddenly, Martin tore forward. Tara wasn't certain what he was trying to do. Possibly knock over the Riprap man? That seemed foolish to her. He was too set and grounded to be blown to the side.

It proved to be a mistake, as the Riprap man managed to get ahold of one of Martin's arms and wouldn't let go.

The Riprap man swung Martin to the side, then swung a rocklike fist at his face, pounding him and knocking Martin's head back.

Where was the killer that Tara had been fearing?

Should she send Soot in? Or Teruko, to get the Riprap man to let go of Martin?

Except that Martin wasn't trying to get away. He let himself be pummeled, again and again, his head jerking back as the Riprap man slammed his fist into Martin's face.

However, Martin wasn't bleeding. Not like how Tara had assumed a human would bleed. His face wasn't cut or bruised, either.

An eerie sound filled the quiet meadow.

Martin, laughing.

The Riprap man tried to strike Martin again, only this time, Martin dodged the blow. Then he grinned at the Riprap man, taking hold of the other's hand.

Tara wasn't certain what Martin was doing to the Riprap man. He appeared to be staring at him, staring him down.

No, wait.

Shrinking him down.

Martin's white skin started to bloat up while the Riprap man was disintegrating. Dust flaked off his flat cheeks. His physical form continued to shrink, until he was a good head shorter than Martin.

Seemed that Tara had made the right call, keeping Soot and Teruko beside her.

The Riprap man tried to let go of Martin's arm, only to have both his hands now caught. Martin held onto the Riprap man's forearms, like some sort of dancer. They started circling again, only much more slowly this time, shuffling to the side.

Tara swallowed hard when she saw Martin's jaw begin to distend. It was like watching an alien horror movie, only it was happening, right in front of her. Martin's face continued to stretch, his jaw growing wider, until it was at least ten inches across. The smell of rotten oranges washed over her, sickly sweet.

Martin suddenly lunged at the Riprap man. The Riprap man ducked, and Martin only managed to wrap his mouth across the top of the Riprap man's head, instead of his full face. Martin's bottom teeth were digging into the Riprap man's eyebrows, while his top teeth were firmly latched into the crown of the Riprap man's head.

A loud, grating howl echoed across the meadow. Tara knew it had been torn from the Riprap man's soul.

She wasn't about to send in Soot or Teruko at this point. Martin had things well in hand.

She also wouldn't allow herself to turn away. This battle had been her doing. She'd made the decision to end the life of the Riprap man before he destroyed all of Portland. She would see this through, even if the sight would live forever in her nightmares.

The Riprap man stumbled backwards one step, then another. Then he managed to find his feet. He picked up Martin and raced toward the edge of the meadow, ramming the other creature's back straight into the hard rock.

The impact jarred Martin's grip and the Riprap man was able to step away. He didn't try hitting Martin again. Instead, he looked up, as if calling for help.

Martin didn't see the danger quick enough. Neither did Tara.

Huge boulders came bounding down the hill, landing on Martin. They were each the size of a small car. Martin was quickly buried.

Martin screamed, a high-pitched wail.

The next rock that landed on the pile cut off the noise, suddenly.

But the Riprap man wasn't finished yet. He used his

hands to start to compress the rocks, pushing them together, both physically as well as magically.

Tara didn't have to watch anymore. She raced away, heading back up the trail before the Riprap man could finish. However, she had no doubt of Martin's fate. He would be completely crushed by those great rocks, pulverized until nothing but a wet slick remained, all his bones broken. She could already hear the crunching sound, different than the sound of boulders grinding together.

Then the Riprap man would be coming after Tara. And she had nothing to either attack with or defend herself, not from that monster.

TARA PANTED AS SHE RACED UP THE STEEP SLOPE. SHE kept looking over her shoulder, waiting for a moving boulder to be rolling up behind her. Soot loaned her feet fleetness, as did her own terror. Sweat dripped down her forehead and pooled at the base of her spine. The sourness of her own fear left a bitter taste in her mouth.

There was nothing she could do to stop the physical form of the Riprap man. His mental presence was bad enough. The original plan had been to engage both, the coven keeping him distracted while Martin attacked.

She felt bad that Martin had been killed, though she knew in her heart that Martin had also been a killer his entire existence.

For now, she just had to survive.

Tara had taken her time when they'd been going down the steep path. It had taken them thirty minutes or so to reach the meadow. Due to the steep climb, she'd expected it to take her over an hour to get back up to the top.

However, even as winded as she was, her legs feeling

rubbery and her insides loose and jelly-like, it took her about thirty minutes to climb back to the top.

The sight of the mud-covered Jeep filled her with relief. She could get there. She could escape. Martin had hidden the keys to the Jeep in the wheel well of the driver side front wheel, as it was much easier to let someone steal the car than to lose the keys in the bush. While Tara didn't have a driver's license, it couldn't be that hard to get herself out of here. Could it?

Tara couldn't help but scream when a nearby rock suddenly transformed itself into the Riprap man.

She still raced toward the car. If she could get it started, she might be able to get away.

The Riprap man came running after her. He didn't move as quickly as she could, even with her recent climb.

Tara raced around the rear of the car, leading him away from the front. While he lumbered around, coming after her, she pulled the keys out. Then she kept going, heading back across the small clearing they'd parked in what seemed like a lifetime ago.

The Riprap man roared his displeasure. He lifted his rocklike hands after her, making a punching motion with his fist.

Tara ducked to the side as a large rock flew past her head.

She whistled for Soot, who started running quick circles around the legs and feet of the Riprap man, forcing him to stop, the strong wind blowing him back.

Tara raced back toward the Jeep. Just before she got there, she heard a loud yelp.

The Riprap man had finally managed to get ahold of Soot. He lifted up the dog by the scruff of the neck, then tossed it over the cliff.

The wind came racing back, but Soot had lost some of his corporeal form.

Tara managed to start up the car, remembering that she needed to put on the brake before the engine would turn over.

The Riprap man roared again. This time, when she looked over, she saw that Teruko now crouched on his chest and clawed at his face, spitting hot coals into his eyes.

Tara spun the wheel and managed to get the car pointed in the right direction, down the forest trail. She couldn't take her eyes off the road as she bounced along. Grasses whipped against the edges of the Jeep. The bright sunlight blinded her as it flickered through the canopy.

She couldn't stop.

She kept feeling as though the road was trying to wrest control of the wheel from her hands. She fought it, fought to stay in control. She sent a quick prayer to Brigid, asking for the strength she needed to make it out of the woods. She also asked Hayyu the goddess of the western winds to blow her foes away from her path, while Samil needed to protect her and guard her soul.

Loud crashing came from behind her. No, it moved to the side, now.

When she glanced to her left, she saw the Riprap man was shouldering his way through the bramble and bushes.

He was trying to get in front of the car. If he made it, he would block her. Running into him would be like driving into a brick wall.

Soot suddenly flew out of the trees from in front of the Riprap man, knocking him back.

Then Soot appeared again beside Tara.

Teruko landed on his shoulders out of nowhere, causing him to fall back again.

Tara realized that she was drawing close to a small creek just ahead.

She called on Mulinohana. Though this wasn't his waterway, he could still help.

All the water in the small creek suddenly rose up, spinning like a hurricane. The Riprap man couldn't avoid the water, and ended up crashing into the middle of it. The water spun all around him, whipping him around.

Tara bounced off the smaller track and onto the larger service road. She kept looking over her shoulder, but she no longer heard him crashing through the underbrush.

Soon, she reached the narrow blacktop, shooting out of the darkness of the trees and into the sunlight. She took a shaky breath and kept going, pushing forward, going as quickly as she dared down the highway.

Would the Riprap man keep after her? Not now, she suspected. She would be safe, at least for a while.

Later tonight, though, would be another matter.

TARA SLOWLY DROVE THE JEEP BACK INTO THE CITY. IT was just after 1 PM. She had already pulled over once and left a message for Lucius, asking him to meet her at Hallowed Ground.

Tara didn't fall down on the ground and kiss the dirty sidewalk, though she considered it as she stepped out of the Jeep. Her legs were still jelly, this time, though, from having to drive for so long, concentrating on something so foreign to her.

At least she'd made it.

"You're sure he's gone?" Lucius said, appearing out of nowhere. "You're quite positive?"

Tara nodded, blinking her tired eyes. "As sure as I can

be," she said. She shivered in the warm sunshine. How did people stand to drive such long distances? Though she'd been sitting for several hours, she was still completely exhausted.

"His family will not be pleased," Lucius said.

"He had a family?" Tara asked. They'd talked about that, hadn't they? Family of choice. Though he couldn't choose one. Would wear people down, eventually.

"His parents," Lucius said. He looked displeased. "How could he be dead? He was older than I was. Much older. I've known him for most of my life. How can he be gone? I would have expected him to outlive us all."

"The Riprap man was waiting for us," Tara said. "In the meadow. We thought we'd have to call him. We didn't."

Lucius nodded. "Well. It will be the last time that thing hurts one of ours," he said. He held out a hand to Tara, seeming impatient.

It took Tara a moment to realize that Lucius wanted the keys to the Jeep. She slowly handed them over to him.

"Where are you going?" Tara asked as Lucius climbed into the dirty vehicle.

"To get reinforcements," Lucius said. "I will be back by eight."

Tara nodded tiredly and watched the elegant man drive away, struck by the contrast between the rough and ready vehicle and the driver.

It took Tara three tries to open the door to Hallowed Ground. Kaede came out of zir office immediately. "You need a bed," ze said, taking one look at Tara.

Tara nodded, though she doubted she would sleep. Or rather, that she would sleep without nightmares.

The crunching sound of bones being broken by rocks followed her all through her dreams.

CHAPTER 6

Vanport isn't well supported. It would be easy to drive all those people out of there. It wouldn't take much to wash that dirty, disgusting place away. The River God could use all the souls who would be lost. Particularly since there's been such a large amount of water gathered in the hills. I've identified the single levee that needs to go. I was once an engineer. Finding that weak point had been the easiest thing for me to do. The more difficult part has been getting Mulinohana to agree to my plan.

Wilson Evermore, Civil Engineer and Scourge of those who don't belong, 1948

TARA WAITED WITH KAEDE AT HALLOWED GROUND UNTIL close to 9 PM, but Lucius never returned. She'd called the rest of the coven, telling them that they didn't need to meet that evening. Kyle had made plans with her to meet the following evening, while Richard had asked to have lunch with her.

She never actually talked with Lucius. Had the Riprap man gotten him as well? It wasn't unusual for all calls to go straight through to his voicemail, as he rarely answered his phone. The being had a singular distaste for talking on the device, and only carried one for convenience.

Heartsore and still tired, Tara went home slowly. She slept better than she would have imagined. She managed to put off any nightmares until three AM, so managed to get a few hours of uninterrupted sleep.

Her morning class went better than she would have thought. Again, it struck her as so odd that everything else was so normal around her while she continued to look at every building she entered, making sure she knew where the exits were, what would be the best place to hide in case of a major earthquake.

Richard met her at a place that did all sorts of different veggie and meat bowls. Tara got a hearty bowl with a lot more carbs than she normally ate, just to build her system back up, a taco salad with black beans, rice, as well as spicy hamburger, sour cream, cheese, guacamole, and lots of fresh greens.

"You look better," Tara told Richard as he joined her at a table. He no longer looked as pasty, and his eyes appeared less haunted. He was in work clothes that day, so a nice gray shirt with thin white pinstripes. It made him look professorial, with his large aviator glasses and lanky black hair.

"You look like shit," Richard told her in return, with a grin to help soften the words. "No, seriously. Are you sleeping at all?"

"Some," Tara admitted. "It's been hard. I've been

worried all the time, you know? And the fight yesterday…" Tara couldn't help but shudder.

"Do you need to talk about it?" Richard asked.

Tara shrugged. "It was bad," she said quietly. She gave him a brief outline of what had occurred.

"Didn't Lucius say that there might be someone else there? Who could possibly help?" Richard said.

"He did," Tara said, nodding. "I'm not sure if the person didn't show up because I escaped successfully, or if they hadn't been there."

"We'll have to ask. If we see him again," Richard said sourly.

"He never promised us that he'd be there for long," Tara said. "And I'm still just hoping he's all right. That nothing happened to him."

Richard nodded. He paused, obviously thinking.

"Spit it out," Tara said after a moment. "You obviously have something on your mind."

Richard grinned at her. "See? This is what I was thinking about. How well we know each other. How well we get along."

"We've always gotten along together well," Tara said. "That's why we're friends." A spike of fear raced through her core. He wasn't thinking about something else, was he?

"Well, we started off dating. We couldn't continue because we were of different religions," Richard said, grinning at her. "But since I've converted, do you think we could try again?"

Tara blinked, surprised but not. Richard was not the solitary type, despite his chosen profession. Though he claimed to be an introvert, he was the most extroverted introvert she'd ever met. He liked people, and talking with people, and hanging out with people. Tara did as well, but not to the same extent.

"So what do you think?" Richard said, keeping his smile firmly in place when she didn't reply immediately.

Tara shook her head. "You know that I adore you, and you're one of my best friends," she said.

"Keeping me in the friend zone," Richard said, nodding. "Any chance I could make my way out of there?"

Tara sighed. "I don't think so," she said after a moment.

"It's because I'm not a witch, I don't have magic, right?" Richard said, finally starting to sound bitter about the whole thing.

"That's a big part of it," Tara said. She shrugged. "But really, I don't think of you that way. I'm sorry."

"It's okay," Richard said. He gave her a brave smile. "I just thought I'd try my luck. You never know, right?"

"You don't know until you try, that's right," Tara said. She reached over and squeezed his arm. "I still enjoy your company, and wouldn't mind hanging out more."

Richard shook his head. "No. I'll need to put up more boundaries. If we aren't getting closer, I don't want to get closer as friends, if that makes sense." He reached over and squeezed her hand, releasing it quickly.

Tara got the hint and took her hand off his arm. She felt bad for hurting his feeling on the one hand. On the other, she couldn't hurt herself for him. That would never work either.

They gave each other sad smiles and finished their lunch. Richard promised to call her later, as well as to stay in the coven, at least for now.

Tara had been so happy with her group, her found family.

How did she prevent it from falling apart all around her?

~

KYLE STILL HADN'T HEARD FROM LUCIUS BY THE TIME HE met up with Tara for dinner at his place. Though she'd moved out, he was still cooking at home more.

Kyle took Tara's coat and hung it in the closet just behind the front door. Tara looked around the familiar condo with curiosity. It had been a few months since she'd been there. She and Kyle still had the occasional movie night, but they'd fallen out of meeting regularly.

The kitchen, immediately to the left, seemed much the same, with stir fry sizzling on the stove and filling the air with the smell of ginger, lemon, and chicken. The rice cooker on the countertop was new, though.

Right in front of her was the living room, with its masculine, leather furniture. It was still in the same configuration, with the long brown couch facing the glass doors that led out to the patio, a small eating nook on the left, and the TV with the comfy chairs to the right.

In the far right corner, Tara saw that Kyle had increased the size of his altar. She didn't stare at it, though she was curious about the carved white statue that now sat prominently in the center of it.

Behind the altar was…something. Tara remembered that before, Kyle had a hidden set of shelves that she'd not really ever noticed. He'd protected it with a distraction spell so she wouldn't pay attention to it.

At that point, she hadn't been a strong enough witch to see through the spells Kyle had put up.

Now, though she still couldn't actually see the shelves themselves, at least she knew that something was there.

"You sense the shelves now, don't you?" Kyle asked as he stepped back into the kitchen, turning the heat back up on the stir fry and stirring as it sizzled back to life.

"I do," Tara said slowly. "I don't mean to pry," she added.

"No, I was curious if you'd finally gained the strength," he said. "I know you couldn't see them when you first passed in, to the circle of water. So I wasn't sure when you'd be able to."

Tara shrugged. "I haven't been studying," she said. "Not at all."

Kyle nodded. "I know," he said as he pulled the wok from the stove. "And we needed to talk about that."

Tara gave an expressive sigh.

"What is it?" Kyle asked. He held up a bottle of red wine, silently asking if she'd like a glass.

"Yes, please," Tara said. Though she rarely drank alcohol, a glass of wine actually sounded really good that evening.

Kyle poured them both a glass then continued serving, putting a large serving of rice in his dish, a smaller one in hers, then covering both with the stir fry. He carried them both to the eating nook. Tara followed, carrying the two glasses of wine and the bottle.

"To old friends," Kyle proposed lifting his glass in a toast.

Tara smiled at him. "To old friends," she added, though she felt deep in her gut that this old friend was also going to ask something of her, something she possibly wasn't going to be prepared for.

～

Tara pushed back her bowl and cradled her wine glass in her hands. "When did you become such a good cook?" she asked. The meal had been fantastic. Kyle had used fresh ginger to liven up the stir fry, as well as some lovely peppers to give it heat. The chicken had been marinated in the lemon juice before being cooked, so it had been nice and savory as well.

"I can follow a recipe, you know," Kyle told her with a grin. "Plus someone may have shown me a thing or two about herbs, you know."

"Yeah, but you were barely cooking when I was living here," Tara told him.

Kyle's grin widened. "Maybe I didn't want you to stay. I knew I'd have to kick you out of the nest sooner rather than later. And if I'd been cooking a lot, you wouldn't have wanted to go."

Tara had to nod. "True, that."

They cleaned up, the quiet falling between them happy and content. Tara almost was able to fully relax.

Almost. She knew that Kyle had something more to say, though. He was just softening her up with a good meal.

And it had worked. She joined him on the couch, looking out through the glass doors into the night.

"How is Soot doing?" Kyle asked. She had called the wind first out on his balcony.

"He's fine," Tara said. She'd been worried about him after his battle with the Riprap man, but he'd come racing to her when she'd finally managed to call him. Same with Teruko.

"Good," Kyle said. "It always surprised me, how you'd managed to tame a wind. And a fire elemental. As well as a water element."

"Yeah," Tara said. A year ago, she couldn't have even imagined doing such a thing. Now, Soot, Teruko, and even Mulinohana were such a part of her life, she couldn't imagine living without them.

"So that's kind of what I wanted to talk with you about," Kyle said.

Tara couldn't help but stiffen in fear. What was her good friend about to ask her?

"Now, I know you haven't been studying at all," Kyle said. "It's getting harder for you to do schooled witch spells, isn't it?"

Tara nodded. "It is," she said. She hadn't wanted to admit it to him. He was one of her best friends, and a schooled witch. He couldn't understand the way she worked with the elements, needing always to follow along the straight lines set out by the laws and lore.

"It's okay," Kyle said. "I'm still here to act as your conscious, whenever you start to abuse the natural magic."

"Thanks, I think," Tara said. She and Ginny tried to keep reign over their natural abilities whenever they were with the rest of the group.

"You're welcome," Kyle said. "Now, I know that Lucius has said that we've been thinking too small. It was why he wanted to try to mesh with the other covens."

"And you know how well that turned out," Tara said sourly. Aaloka, her former mentor, wouldn't even have tea with her anymore. While it had been a remarkable amount of power, the psychic and magical backlash had been severe. Tara and her group had suffered the least. Miss Lucy had let her know that her coven wasn't going to be able to do any magic for a month or more. Aaloka had hinted at the same for their coven.

"I hadn't meant to hurt anyone," Tara said. At least

now they had a good idea why it was such a bad idea to try to bring the covens together. The chances of this sort of fallout were too high.

"I know," Kyle said. "Not just them, but Martin, as well."

"I've never seen Lucius so…distraught," Tara said. "He was really devastated that his friend had been killed."

Kyle gave her an odd look. "I'm not sure that was what was causing him so much grief," he said slowly. "I think that Lucius's pride was hurt as much as anything else."

"What do you mean?"

"He's proposed two solutions," Kyle said. "Neither of them have worked. He isn't mortal. He certainly never sees himself as fallible. Nonetheless, here is where we are."

Tara nodded. That actually made more sense. Lucius wasn't the kind to really care deeply for anyone other than himself.

"Do you know where he might be?" Tara said. She'd asked before, but thought there would be no harm in asking again.

Kyle pressed his lips together. "I may. But I wouldn't tell you, and I certainly wouldn't go there myself."

"Understood," Tara said. "It's just—I'm worried about him. It isn't like him to set an appointment and then not show up."

Kyle gave her a huge grin. "Unless it's to show up at eight PM some other night, and claiming that he meant that time all along."

"That would be exactly like him, wouldn't it? That the misunderstanding was all on our part," Tara said, smiling at Kyle.

"Exactly," Kyle said. He paused, then added, "I'm not worried about him. Not at this point. He's wily, and though he's upset, he wouldn't be stupid enough for the Riprap man to actually catch him. Not yet."

"Okay," Tara said, slightly less worried. "But that isn't the only reason you invited me over here and softened me up with such a good meal."

"No it isn't," Kyle replied, more serious than he'd been earlier. "As I said, you haven't been studying. I know that in order to pass within, to the next level, you're going to need to learn more lore."

Tara grimaced. "Yeah, I know. But do I really need to pass to the next circle? As I said, it's already harder for me to do those sorts of spell. Will learning more help?"

"It might," Kyle said. "And passing to the next level might help as well."

"But why?" Tara said. "Help with what?"

"The next level is the circle of earth," Kyle pointed out.

"And?" Tara prompted when he didn't continue.

"Maybe we've been thinking too big," Kyle said. "Asking other witches and old friends for help. What if the solution is right in front of us?"

Tara still wasn't sure what he meant.

"What if instead of a huge battle, it needs to be smaller? More intimate? Personal?"

Tara made a gesture, urging Kyle to get to the point.

"The Riprap man is associated with the earth, like you are associated with the water, right?" Kyle said. "What happens if we fight like with like?"

Tara still had no idea what her old friend was asking of her.

"What would happen if the next time you met, you had an actual earth elemental to fight against him?"

∼

Tara still wasn't sure what to do with Kyle's suggestion. It made sense in a way. Fight fire with fire, or earth with earth.

She was finally home, curled up on her bed with Soot and Teruko curled up around her. She couldn't ask them, couldn't really talk with them. They weren't that strong, couldn't really communicate with her, not with words. Sure, they still let her know things. But it wasn't human speech.

Mulinohana was her strongest familiar. He took on the form of a person, and could talk.

Ginny had told Tara long ago that part of the problem with hedgewitches and their magic was that it was individual. While the schooled witches magic was weaker, it was more predictable. Tara's magic generally worked about half of the time, and she had no idea how to make it more reliable.

So while Tara could ask Ginny about calling up an earth elemental, working with that type of familiar, she already knew that Ginny wouldn't have any experience with it. Tara already was different than any other witch Ginny had known, having a familiar from more than one element.

Instead, Tara made herself sit up in her bed. Teruko protested, as his purring had already started to fade away as the cat headed toward sleep. Soot just nodded and rolled over, slithering down to the foot of the bed, then laying there like a statue, ready to protect her.

Tara folded her legs under her and leaned against her headboard. She closed her eyes, holding her hands out in lotus pose, then took a deep breath.

She expected that she'd have to fight her tiredness, and would fall into sleep instead of a meditative state. But she found that her breathing smoothed out easily, her mind falling into her body, her thoughts sliding away.

It didn't take long for her to reach a state of altered consciousness. She concentrated on the sound of dripping water, that soft splash that a sink might make, the drips constant and reassuring.

The sound of a louder splash made Tara open her eyes. She stood near the headwaters of the Willamette river. Moss-covered rocks impeded the flow of the water, causing it to make a loud rushing sound. Mud felt cool under her bare toes, while the sunshine warmed her skin.

It didn't embarrass Tara to realize that she'd shown up naked. It wasn't as if Mulinohana were a human male. Plus, much of her craft was done better without the hindrance of clothing.

Still, Mulinohana gave her a bemused smile when he appeared beside her. He looked much as he always did, like a young Native American man in his twenties, wearing his long black hair in two braids that hung down past his shoulders. He was still clothed, wearing light-brown leather vest and no shirt, as well as jeans that had the knees artfully torn out. His bare feet and toes dug into the mud next to hers.

"Thank you for meeting me," Tara said. She paused a moment, breathing in the peace of this place.

"You are always welcome in my home," Mulinohana said. His words never sounded loud, and always seemed to have the hissing of rushing water behind them.

"Thank you also for the aid with the Riprap man," Tara said. She knew that the only reason she'd survived had been because of her familiars.

"That, too, was my pleasure," Mulinohana said. He turned serious dark eyes toward her. "I would not see you come to harm."

"Thank you," Tara said.

When they'd first bonded, Tara had asked him about the process that he'd used to create the Riprap man. It wasn't a spell that she wanted to experience, as it had greatly, though artificially, extended his life.

Fortunately, Mulinohana hadn't wanted to perform it with her. He'd only done it at the insistence of the Riprap man, plus the fact that while Mulinohana had realized that the Riprap man wasn't necessarily a water person, he hadn't at the time realized how much that mattered.

Tara told Mulinohana about her day. She hadn't planned on talking about Richard, but ended up telling the river spirit about him anyway.

"Do you suppose there's a way to give him magic?" Mulinohana asked.

Tara shuddered. "Possibly. But it would be wrong."

Mulinohana tilted his head to one side. "Why is that?"

"That isn't who Richard is," Tara explained.

"It isn't who you see him as, yes. Can you say for certain what is in his soul?" Mulinohana said. "You may want to talk to your friend Lucius about it. He may have some ideas."

Tara nodded. She'd mention it to Richard, then let him decide if he wanted to move ahead. She, however, would also have to make it clear to him that even if he suddenly developed magic, she wouldn't necessarily be interested in him.

Probably. She honestly couldn't say for certain.

"What else?" Mulinohana said. "Surely you didn't come to see me just because of a lover's tiff."

Tara opened her mouth then shut it again, not wanting to try to explain how she and Richard weren't lovers. Then she saw his sly smile, and realized that the river spirit was teasing her.

"Kyle had an idea," Tara said. "He suggested that we fight fire with fire, as it were. Since we know that the Riprap man is associated with earth, would it make sense for me to acquire an earth familiar?"

Tara wasn't prepared in the least for the sudden splash of water that splashed against her lower legs, soaking her from the knees down.

"Why would you come and ask that of me?" Mulinohana said.

Tara took a step back from his sudden rage.

"I am the most important element in your life," Mulinohana said, still angry. "No other familiar you call will be as strong or as willing as I am."

Tara hadn't realized that her water element might be this jealous. She regretted coming here. "I'm sorry," Tara said, trying to back-peddle. "I hadn't meant to insult you. I was coming here to consult you, to ask your wisdom about these things."

"I see," Mulinohana said, though he was barely mollified. "I think it's a dumb idea," he stated plainly.

"But wouldn't you like some help the next time we confront the Riprap man?" Tara asked.

"I need no help," Mulinohana said firmly. "None."

Tara realized that the water spirit would never be able to advise her on this topic. "That's good to know," she assured him. "I will call on you first for our next battle."

Mulinohana narrowed his eyes at her. "The Riprap man is more wily than you realize," he said. "You must take care. It might, maybe, make sense to have more power the next time you meet."

Tara nodded. She thought she understood what Mulinohana wasn't saying: That while he'd never condone Tara enlisting the help of an earth elemental, he still approved it in his own way.

"Thank you," Tara said. She turned to face the river again. Mulinohana stood silent beside her. The rushing water filled her head and carried her off to sleep, finally without nightmares or dreams.

CHAPTER 7

TARA PUT HER TABLET DOWN BESIDE HER ON THE PORCH swing, her head spinning. She'd been trying to stuff so much lore into her brain it actually hurt. Later that evening, Kyle was going to try to use the spell that would help her pass within, from one level to the next. However, she didn't know if she was ready, if she'd ever be ready.

She'd spent the morning working at the Y, and now had a few hours off before putting in more time at Hallowed Ground. Despite the terrible aftermath of trying to mesh the covens, both Sheila and Lucy continued to support Tara's work at the homeless shelter, at least for the time being, by supplying ingredients for Tara and her "teashop".

All Tara had ever wanted to do was to run her own teashop. The one at Hallowed Ground had just stoked that fire, rather than vanquished it. While making teas and sachets for the youth there, what she really wanted to do was to run a business. Feel like a success for a change.

Instead of always feeling as though she was behind in everything, part of the gig culture, working for other people and never for herself.

She might be able to take out a business loan. But that was iffy. She still had her college debt to pay off, would for another five years or more, and she was already approaching thirty.

Some year…

In the meanwhile, here she was studying again. The last few times she'd tried cramming for one of these exams she'd felt as though her brain had been put through a wringer. This time, it just felt like mush.

Was she getting too old for this?

She snorted to herself. Yup. Definitely too old for this saving the world shit. And it just didn't pay well.

She stood up and stretched for a few moments, wondering if she should go for a walk. Her phone rang.

"Hi, Mom," Tara said cheerfully. "What the news from the farm?"

While her parents had spent her childhood in the city of Menominee, Wisconsin, after she'd left home they'd sold the place and bought a hobby farm north of the city. She'd never suspected that her parents would end up being outdoorsy people, but they were.

Her mother launched into a long description of the

garden, what she'd planted, what was still in seed pots. Tara grinned listening to her mother's stories. While Tara considered herself more of a city girl, she certainly appreciated a good garden.

As they finished up their call, Tara realized that yet again, she was facing never talking with her mom again. "You know how much I love you and Dad, right?"

"What's going on this time?" Mom asked sharply.

"What do you mean? Nothing's going on," Tara said.

"Three, maybe four times now, you've gotten morose and needed to tell me just how much you cared for me," Mom said. "It's been happening like clockwork. Right around the time of the equinox or the solstice."

"I can't really tell you about it," Tara said, not wanting to lie too much to her mother, but needing to for her own good. "Let's just say that my life gets really weird sometimes. And it worries me."

That, at least, was the truth. Here she was studying hard to be a stronger witch, to pass within in terms of the circles of power, and to call up an earth familiar so that she could fight someone called the Riprap man.

"You should come and see us, sometime," Mom said. "Soon." She paused, then added, "I could send you a ticket."

Tara knew that her parents didn't have that much money either. But they were at least better established than she was.

"I might take you up on that," Tara said.

"After the summer solstice?" Mom asked.

'That sounds wonderful," Tara said. Hopefully either she would have successfully fought off the Riprap man somehow before then.

Or the west coast would be in ruins.

"I do love you," Tara said.

"I know. I love you to. As does Daddy."

"Thanks, Mom. Bye!"

"Bye."

Tara held the phone in her hand and just looked at it for a while. While she enjoyed being an adult, sometimes she wished she could be a little girl again, let someone else take care of her for a while.

Honestly, that had been the most appealing part of Richard's offer. Not that she wanted a boyfriend or even a constant companion. Just someone to take care of her more often.

Then again, Kyle would cook for her anytime she asked. Ginny would make her teas as well as regale her with stories and make her laugh. Kaede made Tara think, as well as made her a better person. Richard was a dear friend who found things out for her. And Lucius—he brought a wonder to her life, showing her how much else was out in the world, waiting to be discovered.

Tara did have friends, good friends, and a good network.

Did she want more?

And would she be able to answer that by the time the next battle was over?

~

TARA STOOD WITH KYLE IN ROSE PARK, UP IN THE ROSE District. They'd decided that it made more sense for them to do the ritual outside, and not on his balcony, as she'd been calling up earth powers.

It was near the park where Tara had first met Ginny, almost a year ago. Roses lined the edges of the park, as well as grew along the walkways. A few eager bushes had already started blooming, though most would wait until early summer before they'd show their true colors. The wind still carried the scent of sweet roses through the evening air.

Though Tara had thought about contacting the rest of the coven, this was really a private ceremony between her and Kyle. She wasn't about to try binding an earth spirit to her, not yet. This was just the passing within.

Tara and Kyle had already discussed the possibility that she might not be able to pass within, not yet. As she'd managed to call her other familiars before actually becoming that level of witch, Tara tried to reassure herself the it didn't matter if she succeeded or not.

And though she hadn't always been a good student, she had always tried her best, and maintained at least a B average all through school.

Not that an English degree had actually done her much good out here. She would have been much better at a technical school, particularly one that might offer something like a master gardener program.

She'd considered it, but what she still really wanted was to run her own teashop.

Kyle met her in the park, in the middle where all the pathways converged. She saw him walking toward her, then had to look again. For a moment, she thought that he was wearing judges robes. Instead, it was just a black jacket with four long panels hanging off the back, like a ribbon cloak. Fancy knotted frog closures, the kind that were used on old-fashioned uniforms, in black kept the front of the piece shut. Black braid decorated the collar and cuffs as well.

Kyle looked stern, as though he was waiting to pass judgement on her. And he was.

She followed him off the main gravel path, onto the grass nearby. The rose bushes on either side of them appeared to swell up, providing them with privacy. Kyle casually dropped a sachet on the ground. A silence rippled out of it, hiding their words as well.

"We have come here tonight to verify if you are ready to pass within, from the circle of water to the circle of earth," he intoned, his words solemn and clear. "Are you prepared?"

A part of Tara wanted to joke and reply, "As ready as I'll ever be."

But she knew that wouldn't be appropriate. Kyle was taking this seriously. She had to as well.

"I am," she said, holding herself straighter. She was glad that she'd worn something better than just a T-shirt with her jeans, though she doubted her nice, pink and white striped blouse would pass muster with Kyle's fashion sense.

"Then let us begin," Kyle said. "Tell me all the properties of *hyssopus officinalis*," he said.

Tara swallowed. She had a moment of anxiety. Would she remember anything that she'd just learned?

Then the moment passed and she started reeling off the practical, medicinal, culinary, and magical uses of common hyssop.

She could do this.

BY THE TIME KYLE ASKED HIS LAST QUESTION AND TOLD her that he considered himself satisfied, Tara felt completely wrung out. She felt as though her brain was leaking out of her ears. Her tongue had continually gotten twisted on the Latin names for things. Usually, she could figure out the uses, but she'd missed, more than once.

If she'd done this badly the first time, when Aaloka

had been testing her, she wouldn't have passed at all. But Kyle appeared to take pity on her.

"You've acquired the minimum knowledge necessary for passing within," Kyle said. "Now, for the practical."

Tara blinked, confused. He hadn't named a plant. Practical uses for what?

It slowly dawned on her that he was telling her that she needed to perform some earth magic, before he'd try the spell that would pass her within.

"Right. Gotcha," Tara said.

"We can take a break," Kyle told her, his eyes narrowed.

"No, no, I'm fine," Tara lied. "Now, the practical." She thought for a moment. Earth was related to roots, as well as to sex. It was the root of all things. She didn't have to suddenly plow a furrow in the ground between them, though that would be fun.

Instead, Tara reached out and touched one of the nearby rose bushes. She twisted off a branch, ignoring the thorns that dug into her skin. She could heal herself later.

Instead, she held the bush up to Kyle. "Young," she said, touching the pale green leaves. This branch didn't have any buds on it yet. She cupped the bare stem between her palms, pressing her hands together, crushing the thorns into her skin, letting the rose feed from her own blood.

"Older," Tara said as she speeded up the branches inner systems. Buds started popping out at the ends of a few of the stems.

"Mature," Tara announced as the buds began to bloom. The heady scent of roses washed over her. The flowers were the same color as her fresh blood. They fed one another, her life essence seeping into the beauty that supported her soul.

"Aged," Tara finally said as the roses started to wilt,

the petals shrinking as they turned black. Brilliant red hips formed where the roses had been. Tara could smell the sweet, almost tomato taste that they'd have when she used them for tea.

"Gone," Tara added as she pushed the branch all the way past maturity and into death. The leaves went from green, to bearing yellow spots, to blackened, finally drying up to dust. All the green left the stem itself. Even the thorns pushing into her palms turned brittle, snapping off, sticking deeply into her skin.

It was the cycle of life, going from a green growing thing into death, decaying so that something else could grow in its place. That was the lesson that Tara had taken from when she'd walked the circles, the old oak showing her the way to pass through the earth and beyond.

Tara released the now dead stalk and looked up at Kyle.

He held a questioning look on his face. "You're sure that's the way?" he asked her.

Tara blinked. She had always thought of that sort of magic as earth magic. "Yes?" she said, questioning herself now.

Kyle nodded. "That was very powerful magic," he said. "I don't believe it was earth magic, though."

"It is! It must be," Tara said. She'd explained to him about the tree who'd helped her.

He shook his head. "I think that's hedgewitch magic, not lore."

"What was I supposed to do instead? To show roots and a process?" Tara said, growing angry and frustrated. No one ever knew exactly what they'd be tested on, besides the various forms of magic.

"Oh, I don't know. Something simple. Like maybe changing water to wine or something," Kyle said.

His sarcasm didn't make sense to Tara. "What did I do wrong?" she asked simply. "Do you want me to do some other spell? I can try." Her exhaustion was filling her up now. She found it difficult to even stay standing up straight.

Kyle sighed. "I am willing to try to pass you within," he said, holding out his hands. "And while you're very powerful, I don't believe you're at the next level yet."

Tara bit back her frustration. If he'd just tell her what she needed to do, she'd do it!

But they didn't have a lot of time. She nearly reached for his hands, then paused, looking at her bloody palms.

"Just a moment," she said. She picked out the three thorns that had remained imbedded in her skin, the wiped the blood off on the grass nearby.

Kyle looked at her, alarmed. "What the hell did you do?" he asked. He grabbed her wrists and turned her palms up so that he could see.

"I fed the roses what they needed so that they could mature and die," Tara said. She looked back up at him. "Not part of the earth process?"

"No," Kyle said. He kept hold of her wrists, not allowing her to take his hands with her dirty ones.

Kyle called on Areebin first, the protector of souls, then Brigid, then finally Sammil.

The other two times that Kyle had cast the spell to pass Tara within, she'd felt a jolt, then everything cleared.

This time, the shock was clear and sharp, as if she'd just touched a live electric wire. However, instead of the world seeming clearer, she heard a loud buzzing in her head.

Kyle released her hands and stepped back, shaking his head.

"What was that?" Tara asked. She shook her head again. She felt even weaker than she had before.

"I think…I think that we shouldn't have done this at all," Kyle said. "This diminished your powers this time."

Tara nodded. She could tell that.

"It's like you stepped me back, away from the circles I'd already passed through," she said, the hissing noise inside her head turning into a loud roar, as though a waterfall had just sprung up a few feet away.

Kyle nodded. "That's exactly what it seems like," he said. "You've gone too far over into being a hedgewitch," he said. "The schooled witch part of you is leaving."

Tara sighed out loud. Great. This ritual was supposed to help her gain more power, not take away some of what she'd already had.

"What am I going to do now?" she said. She hated the plaintive note in her voice, but magic was really all she had at this point.

"You're going to call an earth elemental," Kyle said firmly. "If you can."

~

TARA SPENT THE NIGHT SLEEPING RESTLESSLY. SHE KEPT dreaming that something was poking her in the back. Was it her powers trying to make their way back inside of her? She had no idea. Every time she turned around, there was nothing there.

Well, except for the one time when the dream turned nightmarish and the ghost of Martin started haunting her. He looked dark, while at the same time, she could see through him to the rock wall behind him, that still held an impression of his shadow. He'd become a simple ghoul, slobbering after whatever life she might grant him.

It was icky and she desperately needed a shower by the time she got up.

She spent the day volunteering at Hallowed Ground. It was good to be reminded that she still had a community. Service went well, and Kaede let her go early so that she might, maybe, perhaps, be able to catch up on her sleep.

At least that was what Tara told Kaede. In actuality, Tara had decided that she needed to see if she could call an earth element on her own.

She'd deeply shocked Kyle with the magic she'd performed the night before. She still wasn't certain why. Was it because she'd used her own blood to fuel the spell? That she'd brought a rose branch from young and growing to producing and then all the way into death? Or was it something else?

He hadn't been able to explain it, and she was still at a loss for what she should have done instead.

Tonight, it would just be her and the gentle earth. Or at least that was what she'd planned on. She didn't know if the Riprap man would show up if she was trying to call an earth spirit. She was tired of running from him, though.

She felt daring, trying this on her own. Maybe it was a dumb idea. Maybe it wasn't. She didn't know, and at this point, she was too tired to care.

Was this the essence of hedge magic?

Tara walked along the river, calling Mulinohana to her side as she ambled. He didn't ask her if she was sure of what she was doing, just walked beside her, lending her his great strength.

Would Mulinohana insure that whatever earth spirit she called would not be as strong as he was? Possibly. But she'd rather have him by her side than put any more of her friends in danger.

They reached a wide spot on the river walk. On the one

side, a steep bank covered in blackberry bramble went down to the water's edge. On the other side, a beautiful fountain splashed.

Tara found herself drawn to the water. She didn't recall seeing this fountain before. It was made out of a polished, brownish-red stone that was speckled with white. The fountain itself was maybe five feet across. A single column rose in the center, fluted along the side. The water flowed out across a flat top with four carved channels in it, splashing down into the basin below.

The water felt cool and soft against Tara's fingers. Her palms had almost completely healed from the ordeal the night before—had some of it just been an illusion? That she hadn't even realized she'd been casting? Or had all of it been real?

Her palms suddenly tingled under the water from the fountain. Tara gasped. When she looked up, she realized that she wasn't in Portland anymore. Or at least not the physical space. Instead of buildings in the distance, all she saw was a wide open field, carpeted in lush summer grass, silvered by the full moon directly overhead. She heard the river behind her, the waters suddenly grown fierce and wild.

Mulinohana no longer stood beside her, but she still heard his voice in the splashing water. She washed her face in the fountain, the cool water tasting sweet on her lips.

Then she strode out into the field, ready to try her hand at the next calling.

~

TARA STOOD IN THE CENTER OF THE OPEN AREA. TREES loomed in the distance, cutting off the rest of the land. In the distance, she still heard the gushing fountain, as well as the rushing of the waters. The air smelled of sunbaked rocks, warm and earthy, remembering the brilliance of the sun from earlier that day.

"I call upon Sammil, the protector of the people, to watch over the rightness of my deeds. Brigid too, hear my prayer, defender of the earth. May the Old Mother moon light my path and keep me away from darkness, and may the wind goddesses Hayvu and Eural carry their righteousness to me."

Tara paused, considering what she needed to do next. She'd chosen a spot that was slightly more bare, where the earth wasn't completely covered in grass.

"I place my hand here," Tara said, easily kneeling and laying her palm against the cool dirt, "and I call to the firmament, to those spirits who are fundamental to us all. I have great work to do elsewhere. Hear my plea and rise to my cause."

Was that her imagination? Or had the ground just trembled?

Tara pressed her will down into the earth. She clenched her fingers in the dirt, trying to draw up a cohesive spirit.

She knew they were there, coursing through the earth like currents in a stream. She could feel the edges of them, but she didn't know how to pull one up or direct it.

"Oh powers of the earth!" Tara called. "I need your aid! Help me prevent the destruction of the west coast!"

A groaning filled the air.

That wasn't her imagination. The ground was truly shuddering.

Tara stayed where she was, kneeling with one hand placed on the earth.

A shadow rose up in front of her. It gained height quickly, growing from knee-height to far over her head.

It was changed into a grass-covered hill, then

continued transforming as she watching, a head forming first, then the body slimming down, until there was a neck, arms, and a torso. It didn't bother rising up above that, or forming legs.

Tara swallowed against a suddenly dry throat.

She'd asked to speak to an earth elemental.

Seemed that someone, or some*thing*, had heard her plea.

CHAPTER 8

> *The drowning of the city of Vanport was so very satisfying. It took less than two hours for the entire place to be wiped off the face of the earth. Nothing of it remains except the mighty river. However, I got too close to the destruction. I let myself be carried away in the celebration of the river. I cannot stay here. My physical body is not necessary for most of the work I do. I have learned how to travel far and do much without it. I will instead set it to live someplace else, someplace safe. Someplace far from the river, where the waters cannot find me. For I intend to live forever, as long as Portland maintains her shining light.*
>
> *Wilson Evermore, Sole Initiate of the Mighty River and Destroyer of Vanport, 1948*

TARA STOOD UP SLOWLY. THOUGH SHE WAS TALL, NEARLY six feet, the creature in front of her was easily twice her height. It had taken on a vaguely human shape in order to speak with her, though the face was covered in grass that shone in the light of the full moon. The air smelled of fresh dirt and grass.

If Tara was being fanciful, she'd say that the creature had grown bangs over its forehead, while keeping the rest of its hair cut short around its ears. Its cheeks were flat and it had a weak chin, reminding her of the Riprap man. Dark holes would do for eyes, as well as just a small bump that worked as a suggestion of a nose.

You ask for help, the creature said. The words didn't reach Tara's ears. Instead, they vibrated through her bones, as if she was listening to the language of earthquakes. Her breastbone tingled as the words passed through her.

"I do," Tara said. "What do you know of the Riprap man?"

Strong, the creature said. *Very strong.*

"Yes. He plans on sending powerful tremors through the earth, enough to destroy all the land along the west coast," Tara said.

The creature nodded, and waved its left hand.

Suddenly, a bas relief map of the west coast of the United States sprang up. Forests wound their way up and down the coast. The major cities were highlighted with bright red lights, while the mountains sprang up blue and cold.

Interesting, the creature said. Fault lines appeared in the map, cracking the earth apart. The city lights dimmed, then bled away. Mountains crumbled. The west half of the map disintegrated. Tara could see it falling into the sea after the earthquakes that the Riprap man would cause.

You want to stop it, the creature rumbled. *Why?*

Tara held herself steady, not taking a step back when the creatures eyes bored into her. "I want to prevent such a huge loss of human life," she said.

Even though the creature was not human, the shrug it gave was recognizable. *You are like ants. More will come.*

"But these lives will be lost. And you will lose many of your hills," she added. How did she impress upon the earth that humans were important?

You would battle instead, the creature said.

"Yes," Tara said when it appeared that it wanted her to answer. "I would stop the Riprap man. Prevent the huge earthquakes."

The creature nodded thoughtfully. *Let me show you.*

The original map fell away. Tara saw a representation of herself suddenly standing in that space. The rest of her coven also appeared. Soot was there, as were Teruko and Mulinohana. They all stood in an open field. Tara recognized the park, close to Hallowed Ground, tall, modern apartment buildings surrounding the small green square.

The Riprap man stood on the other side of the park, facing them. Behind him stood the witches he'd once bound. Tara could tell they were under his control, as they moved in a jerky fashion, and their stare was fixed.

Suddenly, a shape rose in front of the fighting Tara. She recognized it as the cousin of the creature she currently talked with. It had the same weird haircut, the same stocky build, but it also had legs. It was roughly the same height as she was, though twice as wide.

The Riprap man and the earth creature ran at each other. The clash was deafening. They tore at one another, great hunks of earth and rock flying. They both roared. Neither appeared to be able to get the upper hand.

And the ground started to tremble.

Tara and her friends tried to hold the very earth together as the Riprap man and the earth elemental fought.

The coven of the Riprap man still worked with him, channeling their energy into the fault line.

Even before it happened, Tara knew the outcome.

The clash of the two earth elementals was going to be disastrous. Neither of them knew any other way of fighting, than to use and destroy the very earth they stood on.

The ground began to undulate, as though it was no longer solid but made of water. Tara felt sick to her stomach. Solid earth was *not* supposed to move that way. All around the battling witches she saw the nearby buildings start to fall.

Still the Riprap man and the earth element fought on. Their raging fueled the tremors, causing the land to tear itself apart.

It was too late. The Tara in the vision couldn't stop the two creatures. She destroyed Soot, Teruko, even Mulinohana in her attempts to separate the two fighters. Lucius died as well.

The Riprap man and the earth elemental fought on, raging out of the park and into the nearby street. Everywhere they went, destruction followed, a deep fault line that destabilized the earth.

They fought for two days, Tara saw. In the end, at least the earth elemental was successful, managing to smash the Riprap man into pieces.

However, half of the world had been destroyed in their wake.

When the battle was finally over, Tara turned from the terrible sight back to the earth creature in front of her. "Does it have to be that way?" she asked. "Is that the only outcome?"

The creature gave her that very human shrug again. *A chance. A very small chance it works another way.* The creature cocked its head to the left, looking at her. *Are you willing to take it?*

Tara took a deep breath, then let it out, shaking her head.

She hadn't realized how much damage an earth element might do. Particularly when faced with another one, like the Riprap man.

Wise, the creature said. It nodded. *Hope for you yet.*

With a sound like gentle wind blowing through newly fallen leaves, the creature dissolved back into the earth. Tara felt the ripples of its departure deep in the earth. The smell of daisies came to her, slightly sour but bright.

Tara paused for a moment, then she folded her hands in front of her in prayer and bowed her head. "Thank you for hearing my prayers, for coming to my call," she said loudly.

Then she turned and walked back toward the fountain.

Mulinohana no longer stood beside the fountain. She saw his watery face in the bowl, the water from the fountain splashing down on it.

"Did you get what you needed?" he asked.

Tara shook her head. Then shrugged. "Maybe," she said. "I know that I can't fight the Riprap man. Anything strong enough to defeat him will destroy too much. And the witches that he bound are being forced to work for him."

"What will you do?" Mulinohana said.

"I don't know," Tara said. "But I must find another way."

THE QUESTIONS THAT TARA HAD FOLLOWED HER INTO HER dreams that night. She floated on a boat woven out of rose petals. She herself was tiny as well, the bank of the river towering over her head. Each thorn on the blackberry bramble was as long as her arm. She felt she could swim on the scent of the flowers.

Golden words appeared in the water, as if drawn there with fire. The wind kept tugging her this way and that, instead of giving her time to think or respond. She shivered as she tried to steer her tiny craft, but the twig she used for a rudder wasn't solid enough to resist the elements.

How was she going to stop the Riprap man? How could she defeat something so strong, without fighting him? When was he going to strike? She knew they were living on borrowed time at this point.

There had to be something she could do. But she kept going round and round in her boat, never getting anywhere. She felt as though she was circling the drain.

Finally, as dawn started to slide its light around the edges of her window shade, Tara had an idea.

At one point, the Riprap man had been the protector of Portland. He'd gone about it in a strange manner, killing witches and binding their souls to the bridges of Portland so that it wouldn't be flooded again. However, Tara had the impression from Mulinohana that the Riprap man had at one time cared greatly about the city.

Could he be made to care again?

Tara couldn't bind the Riprap man to herself. Even if she had the power, that was just delaying the inevitable problem that would occur when she died. He'd be cast free again and would cause more mischief.

Could she bind him to the city itself? Make him a protector again? Would that work? Could he be made to be a savior instead of a destructor?

Tara wasn't sure if it was possible to change the man's

basic nature. He was a killer, had been one for well over a century, now. What sort of sacrifices would he demand in order to keep the city safe? Whose souls would he demand?

Though as usual, Tara had more questions than answers, for the first time in a long while, she felt as though she might be on the right path.

As Tara was walking toward her MAX stop, heading to the Y for her morning classes, a melodious voice asked her, "Must you really be so cheerful this early in the morning?"

Tara stopped and smiled at Lucius, who'd just appeared beside her. "I'm normally not this cheerful this early," she assured him jovially. "I just might, perhaps, have a plan."

Lucius was beautifully dressed as always, this time in a cream-colored shirt with wide blue stripes and gray trousers. His black leather boots shined as though they'd once been mirrors. He carried his cane with him. As Tara watched, he appeared to be leaning on it more he usually did.

"Does your plan perhaps *not* involve the death of all creatures on the west coast?" Lucius said.

Tara bobbed her head from side to side, as if thinking. "Perhaps," she said.

"Then why are you so cheerful?" Lucius asked.

"Why are you in such a bad mood? What happened? Where have you been for the last few days? We were worried about you," Tara said.

"I shall tell you my news in a bit," Lucius said sourly.

"Though may I assure you that I believe I may have something of a plan as well."

"Good!" Tara said. "Do you want to hear what I've been up to lately?"

"May as well," Lucius said with a sigh. "as I'm assuming that I can't possibly dissuade you from going about your business today."

Tara shrugged. "I have a job," she said seriously. "I don't have enough money that I could just go gallivanting off whenever I feel like it. I need to work in order to make money so I can live."

Lucius nodded. "I've noticed that is a failing with most people. This need to make a living."

"Inconvenient for you, I know."

"Terribly so. But do tell me your adventures, then I'll tell you mine."

Tera told Lucius of her failure to pass within, how she felt as though Kyle's spell to move her to the next circle had actually removed some of her powers, so that she was no longer as advanced with it came to the circles of the schooled witches.

"Fascinating," was Lucius's comment. He actually did look rather interested in her account. "You aged a rose branch in your bare hands?"

Tara nodded, then shrugged. "Circle of life, you know? I figured that was what he was looking for, in terms of the circle of earth."

"I'm sure I wouldn't know," Lucius said. "Strange, though, that he wouldn't tell you ahead of time. Hadn't he prepared a wind for you that first time?"

"He had," Tara said, nodding. An uncomfortable thought occurred to her for the first time. "Wait. You don't think he weakened me on purpose?"

"No, that doesn't sound like our friend Kyle," Lucius

said. "And I know he's still true. No, I think he didn't have anything in mind because he isn't ready to pass to that level yet himself."

Tara nodded, taking a deep breath. Yes, that might have been part of it Kyle was at the same level as she was, in the circle of water. He'd never stepped beyond.

Had it been wrong of them to assume that maybe he could? "Should I have worked with a stronger practitioner? Like Kaede?" Tara said. Though she didn't believe that Kaede knew the passing within spell. Maybe Kyle could teach it to zir…

"You need to ask one of your witches," Lucius said. "I wouldn't know." He paused, then added, "As for weakening you, is that really what happened? Or did Kyle clear the way for you?"

Before Tara could reply, Lucius held up his hand so she'd let him continue. "Are you now a stronger hedgewitch? Now that you aren't as tied down to those circles?"

"I don't know," Tara said. "I don't think that's what he meant to do, at any rate."

Then she thought for a moment. She'd never had such an easy time going into a projected plane before. That she'd traversed so easily with Mulinohana, walking beside the river one moment, then talking to an earth creature the next.

Maybe Kyle hadn't really weakened her after all.

"Was that all?" Lucius said as the MAX train finally pulled up to the station.

"Oh no, there's more, but you'll have to come with me to hear it," Tara told him with a grin.

"Very well," Lucius said.

While Tara was certain that Lucius wouldn't bother with anything so mundane as a ticket, she also assumed that he could turn away any of the transportation cops who might ask for one.

Lucius sat down on the plastic seat beside her with obvious distaste. At least the train smelled more like left over grape gum than the urine from a homeless person.

Tara told Lucius about the night before, and meeting with the earth creature. How it had convinced her that if they somehow managed to conjure a creature strong enough to destroy the Riprap man, it would still have disastrous consequences.

"I am impressed, my dear," Lucius said. "No, really," he assured her. "I have a suspicion of the nature of the creature you spoke with. It does not abide fools gladly. You do realize that you had as great a chance of being destroyed as of it speaking with you, yes?"

"No, I didn't know," Tara said, turning to look at Lucius. "It could have killed me?"

"Easily," he assured her. "But I'm glad it didn't. My adventures sound rather pale in comparison, now."

"I'd still like to hear," Tara assured him.

Lucius looked over at her with a wide grin. "I first tried talking with some of my other brethren. That…didn't go as well as planned." He grimaced and shifted awkwardly in his seat.

Tara's eyes went to his leg. Had Lucius been injured? Had he had some sort of battle with others of his kind?

When she looked back up at his eyes, he shook his head at her.

Seemed that she would never know the full story.

"Since they didn't seem inclined to help us, I went to meet with the other witches. The ones under the bridges. We may have become allies."

~

"LET ME TELL YOU ABOUT THE OTHER COVEN," LUCIUS said. They were sitting at Hallowed Ground, chairs pulled into a circle. He had assured them that they had one more night before the Riprap man would attack. He was waiting for the dark of the moon, which would occur the following evening.

The room was colder than usual. Tara sat with her coat pulled over her shoulders. They'd served some sort of cream sauce that night for service, and the smell of the butter and milk left a sour taste in her mouth. Ginny also seemed to feel the cold, and had two sweaters on. Kyle, Richard, and Kaede appeared to be comfortable in just T-shirts.

"I went to visit Dorothy first, as I felt she might be the most open to my suggestions," Lucius started. "And because I already knew her name," he added, nodding toward Richard.

"It appears that the Riprap man is using them to further his cause," Lucius said. "They are being trained to spread the tremors that he's started, send them out deep under the earth. Not all of them are in agreement with his plan. They know that if they do as he asks, they'll destroy much of the world above them. However, he'll also release his hold on them. They'll be free."

"Do they believe that he'll actually let them go?" Tara said. "Do they trust his word?"

"Not all of them," Lucius said. "Which is why he's had to work so hard at controlling them. If he could have, he would have initiated his plan long ago. He needs their help. So he's had to work at directing their will. He's planning on bringing all the bridges down, in addition to the general chaos."

Tara nodded. None of the bridges had been retrofit with

enough earthquake resistant materials. Only the single port had been upgraded and would possibly survive.

"Fortunately, I have managed to bring them all over to my side," Lucius said with a very satisfied smile. "Our side, as it were. Once the battle is engaged, they will change the direction of their focus from spreading the Riprap man's chaos to stopping him."

"How can you guarantee that?" Kaede asked. "You've already said that they will be under his control."

"It's…complicated," Lucius said. His smug smile didn't decrease in the least. "But may I assure you, we have a good plan."

"And if ye fail, so will the world," Ginny said darkly.

"Believe me, I understand the risks, better than you lot," Lucius said, his manner growing colder. "I will not fail."

Tara glanced over at Kyle. He gave her a small nod. While she understood that part of it was Lucius's pride speaking, she also knew that the being would do everything in his power to succeed this time.

"So we have something of a plan," Tara said. "Or yet another plan. Where should we meet?"

"Where should the battle be joined?" Richard said. He seemed most determined of all of them.

"Here," Kaede said firmly. "It needs to be here. We can protect this spot the best."

"I'm not sure that's what we need," Kyle said slowly. "We need a place we can protect, yes. But we need to actually meet them in battle. They wouldn't be able to even come inside here."

Kaede looked unhappy, but nodded. Hallowed Ground was that protected at this point. Everyone felt it when they walked in. It was probably one of the safest places in the city.

"Do we want to meet at the park nearby?" Tara asked. "That was where the creature showed me we'd chosen for the battle. I mean, we *lost* there, but we were also following a different strategy. That way we'd be close to Hallowed Ground, but not actually on the premises."

"It is a wide open park," Ginny said. "But it's kind of sterile, you know? It isn't a real living space. Not green enough."

Tara found herself nodding. She never would have put it that way, but what Ginny said made sense. They needed someplace more green.

"But I don't want to leave the city limits," Tara said. "That won't work, not with our plans to try to bind the Riprap man."

"We need to be close to the river," Lucius said suddenly. "Near the foot of one of the bridges. That way, we can work better with the witches bound there."

"Mulinohana will be better able to aid us," Tara said. "And probably both Soot and Teruko as well."

"And my winds," Ginny said.

"How about Hayden island?" Richard suggested.

"No," Kyle said after a moment. "Not enough park. We need to be somewhere along the river front."

They finally settled on a park near the Hawthorne bridge. While there would be people around, they felt certain that they could hide themselves well enough.

The location selected, a plan in place, Tara and the others reluctantly said goodnight. None of them really wanted to leave. That would mean that the night was nearly over. The next day would come.

Whether they liked it or not, the next battle would be upon them.

However, Tara had had too many last days and nights.

As she'd said before, she was getting too old to regularly do this saving the world shit.

She ended up walking out the door with Richard, who seemed determined to remain friendly with her. He offered to walk her up to the MAX station.

They shared a comfortable silence as they walked. It had rained earlier, and the air still smelled of wet blacktop. Streetlights reflected orange against the high clouds. Though the night was calm, Tara pulled her jacket more tightly around her.

"So we're doing it again," Richard said softly.

Tara nodded. "Hopefully this will be the final time," she said.

"I wanted you to know that I thought about what you said," Richard said after a few more moments of quiet. "About possibly approaching Lucius, seeing if there's some way for me to stop being so mundane, and maybe acquire some magic."

"As long as you still understand that even if you had magic, that wouldn't change my mind about dating you," Tara felt the need to say.

"I get that," Richard said. His eyes stared off into the far distance. "I really do. And I want you to understand that if I decide to go through with it, it isn't for you. I couldn't make that big of a decision based on someone else. It has to be about me, and what is right for me."

"Good," Tara said. She'd always respected Richard. His consideration made her like him even more.

"I still haven't made up my mind," Richard added after a moment. "I mean, I've already talked with Lucius about it. He said it may be possible, particularly since I've been so involved with the group already, and have an affinity towards, as he put it, the unseen arts."

"Really?" Tara said. She had no idea. "So it's possible?"

Richard hesitated, but then nodded. "It is. He couldn't guarantee it. All he could assure me was that it wouldn't be pleasant. And that I might go mad."

Tara nodded. That actually sounded about right. She'd heard stories in both of her covens about people not being able to handle the power once they discovered it. There wasn't anything anyone could do about it. They had to either come to grips with it themselves, or else, in this modern age, be thoroughly medicated so that they didn't have to deal with it.

"So I might pursue it. I might not," Richard warned.

Tara shook her head. "If we make it through tomorrow, you'll do it," she said.

"No, really, I haven't decided yet."

"Yes, you have," Tara said. "I do know you better than just about anyone else. If you've come far enough along that you're willing to talk with someone about it, it means you've made up your mind. Might not be willing to admit it yet. That's all."

Richard merely shrugged. "I really don't know," he said slowly. He sighed.

"What is it?" Tara asked.

"If I do take on any magic, any at all, I'll never have another Jeannie," he said all in a rush.

"Is there a Jeannie now?"

Richard shook his head. "But it's one of the considerations. Like you, I'm probably not going to want to date outside of my religion, as it were. Which means, if I pursue magic, I'm going to severely limit my dating pool." He paused for a moment. "I'm not like you. I need a partner. Someone to hang out with regularly. More regularly."

"Okay," Tara said, though she didn't really understand. She liked the amount of social interaction she currently had. Didn't need anymore.

"And that's why you were right, keeping us as friends," Richard said. "I get it now. It doesn't have to do with the magic. It's because socially, we'd both have to make a lot of compromises. I get it."

"Thank you," Tara said after a few moments. She'd been worried that he might try to press his luck, or that they'd be awkward together. She really did consider him a dear friend, and nothing more.

"Thank you for still being my friend," Richard said. He bumped shoulders with her. "I need this group as well," he continued. "Who else is going to give me such fascinating research to conduct?"

That made Tara grin. It appeared as though they were healing after all.

As the MAX drew up, Tara turned to Richard and said, "Just one other thing to consider when you're thinking about that dating pool. Most witches are still female. Being a straight male in such a pool may actually increase your chances."

She gave him a quick hug then boarded her train, leaving him still gaping.

CHAPTER 9

Portland is my city. It holds my heart. I've looked over her, protected her, as well as cheered on her progress. However, I must admit that she has grown foreign to me. I am feeling old, suddenly. I watch the trees disappear, the hills sprouting houses instead. I still have the mighty work to do for Mulinohana, keeping the witches at bay, binding their hearts to the bridges so that Portland can continue to thrive. I find myself leaving the city regularly now, for the first time in decades. I've set my physical body in the hills east of the city. The area had been declared a wildlife refuge, so it won't be developed. The path to the meadow is difficult to access. None will threaten me there. I sit in the meadow and look out on the rocks, let the rain fall on my skin, watch the butterflies flit across the grass. Water flows far in the creek far below me. I can just hear the sound of it

passing during the spring. I must admit, as much as the rushing sound soothes me, the cliffs that I watch bring me joy as well.

Wilson Evermore, Long-Standing Guardian and Ancient Soul, 1961

Tara woke early that morning, unable to sleep late.

Today was the day. She and the others would either bind the Riprap man, stop his plans from coming to fruition.

Or the entire west coast would be destroyed.

There still might be some damage. She and the other witches would do their part to keep it to a minimum.

Tara hugged Teruko to her chest for a moment, despite his protests. He wanted to always be the one to initiate contact. Normally she respected that, but this morning, she needed a bit more. He settled against her breasts after a moment, and started up a loud purr.

Soot lay down long her back, spine to spine, warming her up that way. She felt Mulinohana's presence as well, the sound of water splashing somewhere in the distance, like a comforting fountain.

Thus bolstered by her companions, Tara finally felt ready to face the day.

Her classes at the Y flew by that morning. She spent extra time praising the younger children. They would need this warm memory if the world went to hell that evening.

It surprised her that Lucius was waiting for her at her bus stop. "Is everything all right?" Tara asked as she came rushing up.

"You need to go teach because you need the money, correct?" Lucius said, studying her intently.

"True," Tara said. "Though I might teach anyway. I do enjoy it."

"Really?" Lucius said, surprised.

Tara smiled at him. "However, if money were no object, I'd like to open a teashop," she said quietly.

"That makes more sense," Lucius said. "Thank you."

He turned and started striding confidently down the sidewalk.

"See you tonight?" Tara called after him.

"Absolutely," Lucius assured her, waving his hand negligently, not bothering to turn around and look at her again.

Tara made her way into the bus and found a seat. The person in the seat in front of her was eating some sort of spicy potato chips, reminding her that dinner was still a few hours away. She sat on the hard seat and looked out the window. Everyone was going along their business, as usual. Just as she had been. No one knew what was coming.

Then again, life just happened that way. You never knew what was just around the corner. Whether it be the Riprap man or the love of your life.

Tara shook her head and realized that she'd fallen into a funk. The last time she'd thought the world was ending, she'd started making a lot of plans so she'd have something to look forward to, to keep her moving.

She needed to keep moving this time as well.

She pulled up her phone and started looking at real estate sites, searching for commercial space that might work as a teashop.

She was nowhere near being able to fulfill that dream.

But she recognized how important just having the dream was.

~

Alaska and two of the other regulars were waiting for Tara when she reached Hallowed Ground. They were all standing in the industrial kitchen.

"The water's filled for you," Alaska told her. "The cups have been set out. We didn't want to touch your teas, though." She was in all black today, artfully torn and patched, her pale cheeks looking pinched.

"Tonight's the night, right?" Eric asked. He'd been one of her first clients. The calming teas she'd made for him had helped him get better grades in school. He'd grown less pale over the year, more sure of himself, though he was still shy around girls. Tara wondered sometimes if he really liked them, or if he was actually attracted to boys instead and was still figuring it out.

"What do you mean?" Tara asked. She didn't want to lie to them, but she didn't want to put them into harm's way.

"The next fight. It's on," Alaska said, trying to sound much fiercer than she looked.

Tara sighed. "It is," she said slowly. "And I expect you to be safely tucked away in your beds."

Shanice rolled her eyes. She had her hair done in tight braids across her skull, though she'd been threatening to shave it all off, as her feminism didn't have time for your style shit. "Uh huh. So that you can come by and tell us a nice bedtime tale? Not buying it."

"It's going to be dangerous," Tara warned. "And I can't afford to have my focus split, trying to protect you while at the same time defeat the bad guy."

The three looked at each other. "We get that. We really do," Eric said. He gave her an earnestly stubborn look. "But you can't keep us away. We'll stay back, out of trouble. You might need extra help, though. And so we'll be there. Whether you want us there or not."

Tara knew she couldn't argue them out of it. "Thank you," she said. "It does mean a lot to me that the community is so committed to helping each other. I hope we won't need your assistance. It is good to know it's there."

That made all three smile at her, though Eric still narrowed his eyes slightly, as if wondering if this was actually some sort of trick.

"So let's get this party rolling," Tara said, lifting up the curtain on the shelf that held her teas.

THE AFTERNOON PASSED QUICKLY. IT SEEMED THAT MOST everyone in the neighborhood had to stop by for a quick hello that afternoon. Tara had faced the possibility of the world ending by herself before, or at the very least, her world. It was odd to have an entire support network to go through the rough times with her. But good.

After service that night, Tara and Kaede made their way to the riverside park, taking their time and walking through more than one neighborhood as they made their way. Several small groups of people from the neighborhood followed after them. Tara expected that once they arrived at the park, phone trees would be activated and a lot more people would just stop by.

Fortunately, the day had been sunny and nice. A refreshing breeze had picked up as evening had settled in. People rushed by in their cars, hurrying to get to their families. The air smelled of gas and hot sidewalk. It felt good to Tara to stretch her legs, even after working hard all day then standing through much of the evening meal.

"What does Portland mean to you?" Tara asked as they strolled.

Kaede gave her a quick smile. "I've always been attracted to the old buildings," ze said. "The Chinatown gate. The warehouses in the Pearl district. The craftsman houses out in the various neighborhoods. Portland has so many great old buildings downtown still. Like the courthouse. You know?"

"I do," Tara said. She planned on weaving those into the binding spell. Along with the parks and the waterways, which were her first love.

The park was mostly empty by the time they arrived, one last group just finishing up their collective meal. Kyle and Lucius had already staked out the area where the coven would be meeting, close enough to the water that Tara could smell it. Boats passed by as they watched, the sky darkening. The sound of cars passing far over their heads on Hawthorne led a steady beat to the night.

Tara felt the others join them. Even without being in a circle and directing their magic together, just their presence brought a certain hum to the air. In addition, she felt the rest of the community that had gathered, under the trees. They had kept their promise and had stayed far enough away that they weren't in immediate danger. It was still nice to know they were close by, and could be counted on if necessary.

Hopefully, it wouldn't be necessary.

Gracefully, the coven joined together. It was like winds melding. At one moment, they were each their own individual force. Then they braided together, their force multiplying one another.

Tara thanked the gods and goddesses for their protection, their love, their support. She asked for their aid before the great battle, to carry their truth to the four corners of the world, to save the people of the coast.

When Tara finished, she looked out over the river,

feeling the deep currents in the waters. They ran like warm breezes over her skin, down to her fingers.

Then Tara pushed her senses under the earthy, searching for the currents there. She felt them as she had the night before, aware of their existence but no idea how to grasp onto them. They flowed through her fingers like sand. However, she could feel the spot on the earth where her friends stood behind her, prepared like she was.

They were ready. Or at least as ready as they would ever be.

After a final deep breath, Tara began her challenge.

THE GROUP HAD DEBATED HOW THEY'D DRAW THE RIPRAP man to them. Tara had agreed to try Lucius's suggestion first: that she challenge the Riprap man individually.

It was a guy thing that Tara didn't really understand, but she was willing to try.

So Tara reached deep under the earth and sent out a quiet call. A loud one might bring tremors that she did not want.

I challenge the Riprap man.

It was a simple enough sentiment.

She would bet that no one else had ever done such a thing.

I challenge the Riprap man.

Though Tara didn't add the phrase, she still thought about double-dog daring him to show his face.

She felt a trembling in the distance, as if a warning light several miles away had just come on.

I challenge you.

With a great roar, the Riprap man appeared in front of Tera.

She examined him carefully. The body he projected was similar to his physical form. This shape was more manlike, more defined. He had blue eyes and a more human face. Like the first time she'd seen him, he was formally dressed in an old-fashioned brown wool suit and vest, a brilliant white shirt with a black string tie around his neck, and a bowler hat. The smell of wet ropes washed over her, a reminder of how he'd tried to kill her in the past.

Tara felt that she was underdressed suddenly, but she wasn't going to bother changing her appearance. She was wearing a comfortable gray men's T-shirt that fit her perfectly across her shoulders and chest, along with blue jeans and bright red sneakers.

While the Riprap man represented Portland's past, Tara represented the reality of Portland's present day. In addition, she felt that the community, stretched behind her, was really the future, of where the city needed to go.

"Surely you don't intend to actually fight me," the Riprap man said. "You and your little group aren't strong enough." His voice sounded rough, as if he hadn't been using it much lately.

Tara smiled at him. "No. I challenge you for control of the city," she said simply. "You've been the protector of Portland for an age. Time for you to let go and move on."

It was astonishing to her how wide the Riprap man's eyes grew. "You challenge me?" he asked, incredulous.

Yup. This obviously was the way to go.

Tara gave him her most impertinent grin. "I do. You don't seem very interested in protecting the place any more. Time to give it up, old man."

"You think you can do better?" the Riprap man sneered.

"I know we can," Tara said. "You intend to destroy the

entire west coast. We want to save it."

The Riprap man scowled at her. "It's just you I want to stop. To blame. You ruined everything."

"So you're going to destroy the entire place, kill millions of lives, just to get even with me?" Tara said. "You're kidding, right? You know how ridiculous that sounds?"

"You broke my bonds," the Riprap man said. "You ripped apart my reason for being. It is only right that I should destroy everything you love."

"What if there's another way?" Tara asked.

"There is none," the Riprap man said. "Time for you to die."

Behind the Riprap man, the coven of witches who had all been bound to the bridges rose up.

The strength of the blast of power that struck Tara surprised her.

Weren't they supposed to be on her side?

She rallied her coven, keeping their power woven together. She didn't want to blast the witches in return. They needed them. Needed the binding they had to work against the Riprap man.

Tara turned her focus back to the enemy in front of her. He laughed and took a few more steps toward her.

The smell of wet ropes returned. Tara felt them sliding across her ankles. They'd bind her to the earth where she'd be helpless as the bridges tumbled and the waters rose.

No. She would not allow that.

She sent her own binding out to the Riprap man, her winds racing around him. She would not allow him to come closer. He couldn't reach her.

The Riprap man struggled. He seemed surprised by her strength.

He raised one hand behind him, making a gesture,

asking for more.

The witches behind him complied. More power poured from them and into the Riprap man.

He moved one of his feet forward a few inches.

Tara risked looking behind her. What was happening? Why weren't they turning on him?

Lucius still stood there, a part of her coven, woven in with the rest.

However, his eyes had already turned back inside his head. Only the whites were showing. Tara felt his will seeping away. He was a drain on the group.

Instead of bringing the other witches to him, combining the covens, he was being taken over by them. And they were still too influenced by the Riprap man.

Tara didn't want to let Lucius go, release him from the circle of her coven.

She had no choice.

It was either weakening her group, or letting it get taken over from within. Tara released Lucius from the circle, sending him spinning away to the side.

Kaede immediately reached out to the community, drawing from their strength instead to bolster Tara and the others.

It wouldn't be enough. Tara could tell from the grin that the Riprap man gave her.

He was coming for her. Coming for her soul. And he'd take the city with him.

Tara pushed back again, drawing on everything she could. She took strength from the earth as well as the water. She would not go down easily. She pushed the Riprap man back another step, just through sheer force of will.

The witches behind him continued to pour strength into him, continued to bolster his attack.

The ground trembled under Tara's feet. She had to finish this. Soon. Or the Riprap man would end up tearing the world apart.

A warm blast of power nudged Tara's left side.

What was that? Was that Lucius?

Tara risked another look.

By releasing him from the coven, he'd been able to start working on his own again. He gave her a smile, then lifted his hands like an orchestra conductor.

The nature of the power pouring into the Riprap man changed in that instant.

Instead of supporting him, the magic of the witched began to tear at him, ripping away his strength.

The Riprap man tried taking another step forward Tara before he turned his head. Horror crossed his face as he realized what was happening.

The witches he'd bound were suddenly binding *him*.

Tara and her group added to the chains suddenly wrapping around the figure in front of her. They were huge boat chains, each link longer than her palm. Length after length of linked steel, passing around the Riprap man's body and then sinking into the rock.

The witches bound every single part of him, every rock, every muscles, every cell. He no longer had a heart that they could tug out and wrap chains around. Instead, they bound his will. It appeared to Tara like a core of steel, deep within the figure, unbending, but covered in rust and decay. The witches wrapped it in silken gauze woven from their will and desperation, soft but implacable.

The Riprap man roared and tried to escape. He flung himself down into the earth, only to be chased back above ground by the witches waiting for him there. He flew towards the water, intending to swim away.

Mulinohana rose like a water cyclone, unwilling to let

him pass. The river spirit added his own fine lines of water binding the Riprap man's soul, blue and white ribbons added to the chains.

When the Riprap man tried to break free again, Ginny's winds, as well as Soot, kept him in place, not allowing him to step away. Even Teruko helped, setting up a terrible fire that the Riprap man had to turn away from.

And still the chains piled on, until the very figure was obscured by tons of metal links.

With a howl that came from his very soul, the Riprap man came to a stop before Tera. He dropped down onto his knees. Heavy links wrapped around his shoulders. Shackles now covered his wrists. He cried and moaned as he knelt there, his face aged, the stone pitted and flaking.

"I do not want to destroy you," Tara said, stepping forward. Or maybe gliding there, as it felt as though the power she directed lifted and carried her there. "But I will if I must."

The Riprap man raised his face toward her. "I have shown no mercy towards you or your kind. I do not expect any shown toward me."

"Why did you kill the witches?"

The Riprap man managed a minute shrug, the chains rattling. "The river directed me to, at first. They were not worthy of His attention."

"Who else is not worthy?" Tara asked.

"Those who would harm the bridges, hurt the city," the Riprap man said. "And those who have harmed me. Like you."

"Do you wish to become a protector again?" Tara said. That was the heart of the matter.

Miss Lucy was right, Tara might not have the will to actually kill the Riprap man, despite how he'd been brought low before her.

"No," the Riprap man said. "I will not lie to you. I cannot merely live for the city anymore."

Tara thought she understood. She'd seen the wilderness the Riprap man had chosen for placing his physical body. "What if you were to protect not just the city, but all her lands? The trees and forests surrounding her? The waters and the mountains?"

"I would still deal harshly with those who would mean the land harm," the Riprap man warned. "Their souls would still be mine."

Tara wondered if that was good enough.

The witches who had been bound by the Riprap man, who held him now in chains, came forward. "And those who would remain, who would not choose to pass on, we would also judge," they said in unison, a ghostly Greek chorus in the night. "So it would not just be his singular judgement of who posed a threat and who did not."

Tara liked that better. While she trusted that the Riprap man might exaggerate the harm that someone might pose, the witches more level heads. It wouldn't be judge, jury, and executioner, all wrapped into one warped soul.

"Would you be bound under those terms?" Tara asked.

The Riprap man nodded finally. "I would," he said. "For as long as my strength holds me. I would still protect the brilliant pearl of Portland, as well as her lands, from all who would do her harm."

"Thank you," Tara said. She reached for the chains still binding the Riprap man and started adding the places and things of Portland that were dear to her to each link. After she imbued a link, it would pass out of view and into the very body of the Riprap man itself.

The smell of the roses in the city, so sweet and pervasive. Especially the scent of the pioneer roses, that you could track from blocks away. As well as the smell of wet pavement and new concrete, the scent of old bricks and newly waxed floors. Coffee roasting, and fresh rosemary.

The sound of the river in the morning, gently slapping against an empty rowboat tied to a pier. Crickets and frogs sounding off in the mornings and evening, the loud call of a kingfisher as it dove into the water, the industrial sounds of the bees in the blackberry bramble. How the cars swished in the rain, the lonely sound of the train whistle, the chugging of a semi up the steep hills.

Tara thought of all the historic buildings, how long they'd stood, the marble and stone solid against the weather. The beautiful craftsman homes, with their leaded windows and individual designs. The wood that covered them, painted all different colors. The incredible backyards that many of them still had, with mature trees and amazing flowers.

She added in the surrounding wilderness. The feel of the bark of the pine trees, rough under her palms. The prick of the rose thorns. How soft the rain felt when it came in the spring, the chill of the winter that sank into your bones. Soft springy grass under her feet, along with the hardness of boulders and the steepness of cliffs.

The city held all the flavors she loved. Coffee sweetened with honey. Tea with dried blackberries and peppermint leaves. The yeasty sourdough that came from the bakeries in the Pearl District. The way a good steak tasted charbroiled when you went camping. Freshly picked blueberries. Cream and cheese from local cows.

Tara tried to wrap all the feelings and love she had for her city into the binding. She knew it wasn't enough. Just her memories weren't enough.

So Tara reached out to the community who waited

under the trees, asking for their impressions of Portland, to help bind the Riprap man completely.

Wave upon wave of sights, smells, tastes, sounds, as well as the feel of so many things came through Tara, wrapping gently around the Riprap man, tying him firmly to all the good things. The warmth and love of the people, not just the places.

By the time they were finished, the Riprap man had changed. He still had the outward appearance of an old fashioned gentleman. However, the skin of his face had changed, as had his body.

Instead of being made of stone, he now appeared to be flesh and blood. But a modern twist had been added.

Tattoos blossomed across all of his skin. Brilliantly colored scenes of the city intermingled with the rivers, waterfalls, forests and mountains nearby. His entire body was now one singular painting set deep into his flesh. The tattoos flowed up his neck, down across the backs of his hands, and everywhere else.

The Riprap man staggered up to his feet, swayed for a moment, then he found his strength and stood proud and tall.

Tara could feel the way he reached his roots down, into the very land itself, feeling the firmament on which the city had been built. His gaze reached up to the underbelly of the bridge they stood beside, then past it, to the clouds. He looked all around himself, turning a small circle.

"This is…different," he said slowly.

His voice sounded much more melodic than Tara had ever heard it. She still caught the scent of wet ropes, but also of spring roses.

For the first time, the Riprap man gave Tara a real smile. "I could get used to this," he said softly. He banished his hat and jacket. A much younger man suddenly stood there, almost modern looking. "You can call me Wilson." he said. "Wilson Evermore."

"I am pleased to meet you, Wilson Evermore," Tara said. She strode forward and held out her hand.

Wilson paused for a moment, then reached out and shook it firmly. "No one has addressed me by that name in over a century," he said softly. "Thank you."

Tara nodded. He'd lost his name so long ago. What sort of man, being, protector, would it describe now?

The coven of witches that the Riprap man had once bound started drifting forward. One by one they touched him. Some of them disappeared slowly, leaving their long stasis and traveling forward to whatever the next place was for them.

Others, though, touched him and suddenly took on a stronger form. Some of the ink flowed out from Wilson, wrapping around their skin. They took on purpose and place beyond the bridges where they'd been bound, five witches in all.

It was a formidable force, Tara recognized. Instead of threatening each other, they could now all work together.

A community.

She felt her own coven form around her, stepping forward to see what they'd created. Ginny's winds appeared to be celebrating, dancing from one end of the line to the other. Kaede held out zir hands in welcome. Tara understood that ze was opening up Hallowed Ground to them, whenever they needed a respite. Kyle bowed to them, and she heard him pledging his use of law to uphold their decisions and to protect the lands as well. Richard vowed to answer any questions they may have, research whatever it was they needed.

Lucius granted them the ability to call on him if there was ever a great need.

The people behind them also stepped forward, pledging to do their part, to further the effects of the protectors. To heal Portland as much as was in their ability.

Tara finally spoke again. "Thank you, thank you, thank you. I cannot express how much joy this brings me."

Wilson gave her a huge smile. "I'll be seeing you," he said before he faded away with the other witches.

Tara couldn't help but grin. Finally, she'd be looking forward to his visits.

As well as the rest of her much more peaceful life.

~

"IT WOULDN'T BE THAT DIFFICULT," LUCIUS ASSURED Tara.

She looked around the empty space, dubious.

For the past week, since the final battle, Lucius had been insistent that Tara accompany him to various commercial sites available for rent, trying to find the location for her eventual teashop.

Lucius had promised that he would loan Tara the money to start up her shop for as long as she needed it. It seemed like such a large outlay to her, as well as a huge project. And what if she failed?

But Lucius wouldn't hear any of her excuses, and just dragged her to the next location.

Tara just wasn't sure she was ready for this. Though as Lucius had pointed out, if not now, then when?

The most recent shop he'd brought her to might actually work. It was zoned for commercial and had been a retail shop at one point. A built-in counter was on the left, a few feet from the door. Wide windows looked out on a street. As it was near a university, there would be plenty of foot traffic.

Tara had determined that she wouldn't cook on the premises, and instead, would just sell others' goods. She already had the contact information from a number of different suppliers.

The amount of the loan worried Tara the most. Not just for renting the location, but for fixing it up, buying all her supplies, doing advertising, hiring staff. Kyle had assured her that Lucius would keep his word, and would never hound her for the remainder of it. The amount of interest was miniscule as well. And the contracts would have provisions for if Tara got behind in her payments, allowing her to step out of her obligations gracefully.

At least she'd gotten Lucius to agree that she needed to start small. At first, he'd been taking her to huge restaurant spaces, with over two thousand square feet of space. Finally they'd started visiting much smaller locations, more like two hundred sqaure feet. And he'd had to learn about locations as well. Putting up a shop out in the middle of the a suburban shopping mall, while she could charge a lot for her teas, wouldn't be right for the type of shop she had in mind.

This place, though…Tara turned silently in the space. She could already see the clean white chairs and tables that would take up most of the floor. There would be a corner over there for kids, with lower tables and maybe a basket of toys or games. Power strips would have to be added along the walls, so students could come in and work. She'd have to set hours, so that students didn't hog the tables but would willingly pay "table rent" as it were. One of the things that Richard had suggested was setting up the WiFi so that the password changed after someone had used it for a couple of hours.

Lucius stood there like a proud papa. "This is the longest you've spent in any place I've taken you," he said when she finally looked over at him. "Dare I hope that you might decide to take a chance on this?"

Tara sighed. It still seemed like so much. But she wasn't afraid of hard work.

Her mom and dad had also offered to help. As they'd grown so handy over the last decade or so, she knew that she could rely on them, and they'd actually be a help when they came out to visit.

Plus, she had a community now. So many of the teens from Hallowed Ground would be fighting for a chance to work in her teashop. They run fliers for her, spread the word to all their friends. They'd be there for whatever needed doing.

Tara looked around the empty space again. So much potential. So much hope.

If she was only willing to take the chance.

"Shall we?" Lucius said, a big grin on his face.

"I'm still not sure what you're getting out of this deal," Tara said, even as her heart was already starting to settle into this new space.

"I will not be with your coven for that much longer," Lucius said seriously. "You've done the most important, incredible work. Much more than I've ever thought humans could achieve, particularly in such a short amount of time."

"Thank you, I think," Tara said.

"You gave me a space," Lucius said. "I truly appreciate that, more than you know. I wasn't drifting, my kind don't drift or have the need to 'find ourselves' as you so quaintly put it. But we do need to pause now and again, dip our toes back in the stream of life before moving on. You gave me that experience."

"You're welcome," Tara said. She thought she understood. Lucius was as close to an immortal being as she'd ever met. It made sense that he'd float away from society now and again, then get closer for a time.

"So I wanted to return the favor," Lucius said. "Give you your own space. See what other amazing antics you might get up to with a modicum of support."

"I appreciate it," Tara said.

"But?" Lucius said with a heavy sigh.

"So," Tara said, "I'd like to take you up on your offer."

"Really?" Lucius said, sounding amazed and pleased.

"Really," Tara said.

It was time for her to have her own space to protect, to grow, to love.

RICHARD DECIDED TO PASS ON LUCIUS'S OFFER OF SEEING if he could pick up some magic. It was too big of a leap for him, to give up being fully mundane and possibly become something else. The risks were too great as well.

The following week, he also started dating someone new. He said he'd just needed a push, and thanked Tara once again for turning him down.

Kyle shyly showed up at the coven's next picnic with a date, a tall black man who had a ready smile and a hearty laugh. Tara had never seen Kyle be physical with anyone before, and was fascinated with them holding hands. She hoped it would work out for them.

Ginny turned out to be Tara's first hire for the teashop. Like Tara, she had a knack for creating the perfect, bespoke tea for a customer. She also had a better knack for hiring people than Tara did, so the teashop was quickly staffed with the perfect combination of people.

Tara still volunteered at Hallowed Ground, though she cut down the hours. Kaede found other people to man

Tara's "teashop" in the community center, an older couple who were great with the teens, and able to give them what they needed, even if there was no longer any magic involved.

The tea shop, which Tara had very imaginatively called, "Tara's Teashop" had been open for three months before Wilson found the shop.

He looked much younger than the last time Tara had seen him. He still wore a long-sleeved shirt, despite the summer heat. But he also wore shorts and sandals, showing off muscular, tattooed legs. The colors of his tattoos were still amazing, as if they were all brand new.

Tara took one look at Wilson and reached for the purple heather, adding it to wild mint and tossing in a sprig of lemon thyme. She steeped it, then served it over ice for him, with a splash of lemonade and a hibiscus vinegar shrub.

"Thank you," Wilson said, raising his glass to her. He sipped it, then his eyes grew wide in surprise. "That's lovely," he said. He smiled, then added, "It tastes like a wonderful combination of old and new."

"Good," Tara said. She was about to step out from behind the counter to talk with him when one of the staff called her name.

When she turned back, Wilson was gone.

No matter. She knew that he'd blessed her shop, blessed her place, just as he was doing for every place he traveled to.

There were a lot of places for him to go to. The witches, as well.

Tara went back to work, content for the first time in a very long time.

The future was finally truly bright, not just for her, but for the region and everyone she loved as well.

CHAPTER 10

> *After living in the city for so long, it's strangely freeing to be able to just wander. To go to the countryside, be in the foothills and forests that I adore, then travel back to concrete and lights. Portland continues to thrive. Not everyone can see it, but I can sense the glimmer of a greater plan. The community will come together, not in the short term but generally, overall. The witches I work with ensure that the right people are starting to find their places. The crowning moment of glory won't come for a few generations. Ah, but then? Such a bright light will shine from this small city, over the entire world. And though I will do my part, and will have to work hard, I will continue to bless the name of my benefactress who has put me on the right path finally: Tara.*
>
> *Wilson Evermore, Protector of the Greater Portlandia and the Former Riprap Man*

READ MORE!

Be sure to read all the books in The Witch's Progress Series!

Circle of Air
Circle of Fire
Circle of Water
Circle of Earth

ABOUT THE AUTHOR

Leah Cutter writes page-turning fiction in exotic locations, such as a magical New Orleans, the ancient Orient, Hungary, the Oregon coast, rural Kentucky, Seattle, Minneapolis, and many others.

She writes literary, fantasy, mystery, science fiction, and horror fiction. Her short fiction has been published in magazines like *Alfred Hitchcock's Mystery Magazine* and *Talebones*, anthologies like Fiction River, and on the web. Her long fiction has been published both by New York publishers as well as small presses.

Find Leah's books on Knotted Road Press at (www.KnottedRoadPress.com)

Follow her blog at www.LeahCutter.com.

Reviews

It's true. Reviews help me sell more books. If you've enjoyed this story, please consider leaving a review of it on your favorite site.

Come someplace new…
Are you a traveler? Do you enjoy exploring strange new worlds, new cultures, new people?

Journey into the various lands envisioned by Leah Cutter.

Sign up for my newsletter and I'll start you on your travels with a free copy of my book, *The Island Sampler*.

I will never spam you or use your email for nefarious purposes. You can also unsubscribe at any time.

http://www.LeahCutter.com/newsletter/

ABOUT KNOTTED ROAD PRESS

Knotted Road Press fiction specializes in dynamic writing set in mysterious, exotic locations.

Knotted Road Press non-fiction publishes autobiographies, business books, cookbooks, and how-to books with unique voices.

Knotted Road Press creates DRM-free ebooks as well as high-quality print books for readers around the world.

With authors in a variety of genres including literary, poetry, mystery, fantasy, and science fiction, Knotted Road Press has something for everyone.

Knotted Road Press
www.KnottedRoadPress.com

www.ingramcontent.com/pod-product-compliance
Lightning Source LLC
Chambersburg PA
CBHW070656100726
47907CB00007B/2229